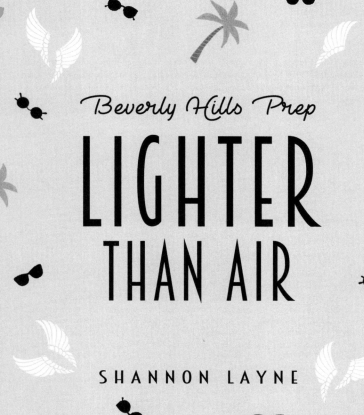

Beverly Hills Prep

LIGHTER
THAN AIR

SHANNON LAYNE

EPIC Escape

An Imprint of EPIC Press
abdopublishing.com

Lighter than Air
Beverly Hills Prep: Book #3

abdopublishing.com

Published by EPIC Press, a division of ABDO, PO Box 398166, Minneapolis, Minnesota 55439. Copyright © 2019 by Abdo Consulting Group, Inc. International copyrights reserved in all countries. No part of this book may be reproduced in any form without written permission from the publisher. Escape™ is a trademark and logo of EPIC Press.

Printed in the United States of America, North Mankato, Minnesota.
052018
092018

Cover design by Laura Mitchell
Edited by Ryan Hume

Library of Congress Cataloging-in-Publication Data

Library of Congress Control Number: 2016962590

Publisher's Cataloging in Publication Data

Names: Layne, Shannon, author.
Title: Lighter than air/ by Shannon Layne
Description: Minneapolis, MN : EPIC Press, 2019 | Series: Beverly hills prep; #3
Summary: Marina is a member of the school dance team that has only limited spots available in the annual spring showcase. Feeling more pressure than ever to perform, the school administration forces her to go to counseling for an eating disorder. All Marina cares about is her performance in the showcase—but will her disease get in the way of her dream?
Identifiers: ISBN 9781680767100 (lib. bdg.) | ISBN 9781680767667 (ebook)
Subjects: LCSH: Dance teams--Fiction. | Eating disorders--Treatment--Fiction. | Private preparatory schools--Fiction. | Teenage girls--Fiction | Young adult fiction.
Classification: DDC [FIC]--dc23

For any girl who has ever looked in the mirror and wished for something different than her own reflection.

*Nothing can dim the light
that shines from within.*
—Maya Angelou

Chapter One

She needed everything to be pink.

Having a bubble gum-colored comforter and a rosebud blanket wasn't even close to enough. Marina wanted the walls painted fuchsia, even the ceiling. Her sheets were dusty pink, her carpet was a soft blush, and even her dresser was repainted in raspberry. As a little girl it was the most perfect place she could imagine. Her mother always wore a pink nightgown when she tucked Marina in. It was silky and trimmed in lace and it always peeked through her mother's bathrobe and Marina couldn't think of a color more beautiful. She wanted everything to be that color. Her room, vibrant as it was, made her happy. The tiny ballet shoes and the worn-out leotards stuffed into her pink dresser made her happy.

Her mother loved taking her to ballet class. She always smiled when she walked Marina through the doors—parents were discouraged from coming all the way inside; the shiny floors were reserved for the girls in tutus and their instructors. Marina knew she wasn't the best one in the class, but she paid attention when other girls got distracted, and she always pointed her toes. Her mother had been a ballerina, and on the days when the parents were allowed to watch the classes, she always came to see Marina.

"You look so perfect in your leotard," her mother would say as they got ready for class and she pulled Marina's dark hair tight into a bun. "You remind me of myself when I was little."

Marina had seen the photos though, of her mother, and they didn't look the same to her. Her mom was taller, with longer legs and slimmer arms, and Marina was round as a pancake. She tried standing taller, stretching her neck toward the sky, hoping she would start to look like the girl in the photos. That was all she really wanted.

Chapter Two

"Do we all really have to wear the exact same leotard for practice, too?" complained Marina's freshman roommate, Lulu. "We already have to match every single day of our lives with our stupid uniforms."

"You've only been here for a few months and you're already tired of the uniforms?" said another girl.

"They're just so boring. I hate plaid."

Marina stretched her arms over her head, still breathing hard. She grabbed her inhaler and turned away from the other girls to take a deep breath and then release, her heart rate finally slowing. Dance team practice had just ended and Marina's asthma was acting up again. Lulu liked to complain, but most of the time Marina didn't mind. It was easy to nod along to her babbling without really paying attention to what she was saying. Marina had gotten used to it since the start of school. Lulu seemed to hate everything about Beverly Hills Preparatory Academy, but Marina was a second year now and she loved everything about it, from the brick and ivy front doors to the cavernous ceilings of the library and the chandeliers in the common rooms. School had just started again after Christmas break and Marina was so happy to be back she could've slept in her blazer.

"I like our uniforms," she said now. "Last year when I was a freshman we had to wear blazers every single day. Now they let us just wear the button-downs."

"I just want to wear jeans."

Marina hated jeans, and the way they seemed to make pockets of fat appear out of nowhere on the backs of her hips. It always felt like they were strangling her. She sighed. It would be so much easier if they would've just put her with another second year, but the girl she'd lived with last year had transferred or gone to fat camp or something. That didn't really matter to Marina—girls left because of stuff like that all the time, first of all. But more than that, it wasn't her dumb roommate she'd wanted to be friends with.

The most popular girls in school were a group mostly on the gymnastics team mixed with a few others—Vivienne, Annabelle, Victoria, Roxy, and Lulu, her new roommate. All Marina wanted was for them to like her. Last year, she felt like none of them had really noticed her. She'd been just a freshman in the back row, nothing special, but now Marina was a second year, and Lulu's roommate, and she was determined to make them all see she'd be a perfect fit in the group. It had only been a couple months since school started and she thought she was definitely making progress.

"Alright, girls, gather up," said the dance instructor, Ms. Bennett. "I have a few updates about the spring showcase."

Marina perked up. The spring showcase was a huge event put on by the school, geared mostly toward the seniors, but with a limited number of slots available for younger dancers to perform. Marina had gotten a spot onstage last year, but only for the shortest number. All in all, she'd probably only gotten twenty seconds in the bright lights of the stage. Still, she'd never been able to get enough of that feeling, the one she got in the spotlight. It had been that way since she was a little girl. When she was young, and all the rest of the dancers had been chubby and short just like her, she'd gotten as much time under the lights as everyone else. But as she got older, competition grew fiercer, and now Marina had limited amount of time as the star. Everyone just seemed to be able to pirouette just as many times as her, or more, and everyone's legs seemed to go a little higher. Marina practiced more than anyone she knew, every single day, most of the time, and it seemed like other girls barely tried at practice and were still edging her out of positions.

Marina twisted her skirt and listened to her

instructor, making her way forward from the back of the group so she could hear Ms. Bennett clearly.

"The spots for this year will be even more limited," said Ms. Bennett. "Seniors are guaranteed to be in at least one of the shorter numbers, but the rest of the spots are up for grabs for the rest of you."

"Why are they more limited?" asked Lulu.

"We have more seniors on the team than last year, and the school is also cutting the time allotted for the showcase. The tryouts for performance slots will be tougher for younger classes—sorry about that, but that's the way it goes. Now, all of you get back to the dormitories before lights out. Day students, see you tomorrow night."

Marina's throat tightened, and she grabbed her inhaler again as she headed to the dorms behind Lulu and the rest of the resident students on the dance team.

Less time? More seniors? Marina wanted to throw up. She'd barely made it onstage last year—how was she supposed to do that again against greater odds?

I'll just have to try harder, she thought as the group

walked from the on-campus studio toward the dormitories. The dance studio was yet another separate annex on campus. Marina's father had donated most of the money for the remodel of the building years before Marina was even accepted to Beverly Hills Prep, he'd been so sure she'd get in. Still, it had been close— Marina had been wait-listed for almost a month before she'd been admitted, and it was the most miserable month of her life. Finally, her dad made a call to the administrative office and got it all straightened out. Marina would never tell anyone that.

Lulu took out her key to their room as the two split off from the group. Marina could hear girls talking in the common room down the hallway, so she knew they still had a little time before lights out. With a sigh, Lulu flopped down on the couch in the living space of their dormitory. Marina had specifically requested the Meadows dorm her first year, because she'd heard it was the most popular, but she'd ended up in Oceanside. Oceanside was right next to Meadows, though, and you could see the arboretum from Marina's window, so she figured it was just as good.

"Hey," said Bridget, poking her head into the door. Bridget had frizzy blond hair and buck teeth and her room was a few doors down. "Do you guys wanna come to the dining commons before lights out? The cooks will give us the leftover cinnamon rolls if we ask."

"Ugh, yes," said Lulu, "I'm starving."

Lulu had legs that looked to Marina like twigs, or even blades of grass—they were so tiny. But Lulu ate like a teenage boy. Marina didn't understand how that was even possible.

"I shouldn't," said Marina, thinking about how her leotard was feeling a bit tight through the waist. "I had such a big dinner."

"Oh, come on," said Bridget. "One little cinnamon roll isn't going to hurt you."

Lulu was already out the door, and Marina didn't want to miss out. Lulu might complain a lot, but at least she was talking—when they'd first moved in together, Lulu had just shot Marina weird looks for weeks until she decided she was worthy of a conversation. Marina hated being in a quiet room. She had six younger brothers and sisters, so she was used to noise, and she could sleep through a hurricane.

The cinnamon rolls weren't "little," at all, as it turned out. The one the cook handed to Marina was practically bigger than her head, and drizzled in melted caramel.

I'll just have one bite, thought Marina as she licked her fingers. *No big deal.* Lulu was already halfway done with hers.

"Did you guys hear about Nora?" said Bridget as they walked back down the hallway. "Passing out during the faculty discussion in the auditorium? What is that about?"

"I heard she has a secret seizure condition she doesn't tell people about," said Lulu. "That's what happened."

"Really?" said Marina.

"That's just what I heard."

"Wasn't she seeing that guy she met at the dance?" asked Marina.

"I'm not sure," said Bridget. "I thought so, but I don't think she's seen him lately."

"That's her loss. That guy was so cute," said Lulu. "Whatever. Maybe she's more into girls, like that girl on the field hockey team."

"Wait, what?" said Marina. "Jeez, why does no one tell me these things?"

"You're just always behind," shot Lulu. "It's only winter and this school is already up to its ears in drama. I love it. It's way more interesting than my old school."

"It has been crazy," said Marina. "I don't remember it being like this last year, but I was just a freshman then so I could've been missing things."

Lulu tossed her hair over her shoulder. They both waved goodbye to Bridget as they re-entered their room, Lulu licking her fingers clean as Marina finished off the last bite of her own roll. She was already filled with regret; her tummy felt like it was going to burst and she was jittery from all the sugar.

"'Night," said Lulu, and before Marina could respond, Lulu's bedroom door slammed shut.

Chapter Three

Marina walked past the cream-colored couch and the braided navy rugs and into her own room on the other side of the common area. It was nearly as pink as the one at her house still was, but she'd tried to tone it down after her roommate from last year made fun of her. Instead of the raspberry comforter, she had chosen one of tasteful blush, nearly beige, and her dresser was white with just a corner of painted roses. She'd even left the walls in the pure white of the original paint instead of trying to convince the administration to let her paint them hot pink.

She'd hung photos of her family, from the babies to a favorite portrait of all of them together, in black and white on the walls. Some of them she'd taken herself, especially the ones of the babies. Her youngest brother was barely two years old and she'd lain on her stomach for nearly an hour just to get the close up of him smiling. Marina made a mental note to call her mom back; they normally talked every single day, or close to it, but she'd missed her call today, somehow. Marina's stomach churned, still painfully full from the cinnamon roll, and she winced. She wished she could take back the decision to eat it at all.

Her freshman year she'd come in without a clue of what it would really be like to eat in the dining halls, with the food their professional chefs cooked for them. Not that her mama didn't make delicious food for her at home, she did, but she was always there to make sure Marina took the right portion and didn't stuff herself. Her first few months at this school, Marina had eaten so much at dinner every night that she'd fall asleep as soon as she got back to her room. It made things easier.

She was lonely, and away from her family for the first time, and eating just helped her feel calmer. Her family lived in Anaheim Hills, so really she wasn't far from them at all, but sometimes Beverly Hills Prep felt like an entirely different world.

When she came home for the summer after her freshman year, her mother had gotten her on a diet almost immediately. Marina hadn't minded—having someone to police her actually helped her feel more in control. She'd dropped most of the weight, but when she'd come back to start her second year, it had immediately started to cling back on again. She couldn't seem to help it. The handmade cinnamon rolls and the cheesecake bars with their buttery graham cracker crust just called to her. Even the Bolognese pasta she loved at dinner and the buttered, flaky croissants she ate at breakfast were all conspiring to make her middle rounder by the day, it seemed. She was also growing addicted to the hot cocoa with heavy whipped cream from the beverage cart just outside the dining hall. It should be illegal to melt chocolate chips into drinks that way.

As Marina got ready for bed, she stood in front of the mirror and turned slowly, assessing her body from every angle. Her legs were still okay, tanned and slim from a summer spent out on the boat in the harbor, and her arms were strong. All she needed to do was get rid of the fat around her middle, and she'd be fine. Marina poked her tummy, imagining she saw fat that wasn't even really there. Her own body expanded in her mind, her thighs growing wider, her middle even fuller. She started to panic.

Tomorrow, the diet starts again, she told herself. *I can fix this. No more cinnamon rolls.*

Feeling more positive already, Marina stepped into the shower and let the hot water rush over her tired muscles. She had a quiz tomorrow that she had barely studied for, but it was just on the reading and Marina hated reading. It always gave her a headache and she seemed to forget what the line had been about as soon as she finished it. She'd get by like she usually did, but she was just never going to be a star scholar or anything like that. That didn't bother her at all—all she wanted was to end up just like her mom with a big family and a husband she could trust to take care of the business aspects of things.

Marina's dad was almost never home. He was always either at the downtown office in Los Angeles, or traveling. He'd been a corporate lawyer when she was younger, and technically still was, but now he was a partner in the firm and was more likely to be spending time in board meetings than scheduling clients. He was always saying to Marina that she needed to get her head out of the clouds, spend more time in the library and less at the barre, but Marina couldn't think of anything she'd want to do less than follow in her dad's footsteps. She loved him, but she wanted to be at home and raise children, or be a dancer. Anything but sit in an office all day and talk on the phone and have to memorize all those laws and statutes.

Marina stepped out of the shower, toweling off with her favorite strawberry-pink towel, and then slipped on her fuchsia pajamas as the dorm heads began calling for lights out.

●●

The next morning, Marina skipped breakfast instead of getting up and going to the dining hall for her usual breakfast of eggs Benedict, or blueberry-lemon pancakes, both usually with a few sides of pastries. As a result, she was irritated and cranky by the time lunch rolled around, and all she could think of during the stupid quiz was the sandwich she was going to make in the dining hall. She hurried there as soon as her last morning class came to a close, her stomach rumbling as she headed for the front of the line.

"Hungry today, Marina?" said Chef Leonardo when she asked for both the paprika-sprinkled potato wedges and four-cheese Italian-style macaroni, but his smile was so kindly Marina didn't feel embarrassed.

"Yeah, I'm starving," she admitted as he handed her

a cup of the gourmet macaroni. "I didn't get a chance to get to breakfast this morning."

In line in front of her, she could see Lulu making her own sandwich at the building station. She was chatting with Roxy, from the gymnastics team. The two had gone to middle school together and were old friends, even though Marina thought Roxy was way too sweet to be so close to someone like Lulu.

"Hey, guys," said Marina, grabbing a soda as she walked up to them. "Is it cool if I sit with you?"

Roxy smiled at her, and Marina thought she saw her nudge Lulu with her elbow.

"Sure," said Lulu tightly. "We're just sitting with the rest of Roxy's team and the girls from dance over there." She gestured toward a table in the back corner.

"Sounds good," said Marina. She walked in that direction, gingerly balancing her full tray before sitting down next to a dance teammate. Across the table she could see Annabelle from the gymnastics team whispering something to Victoria, her best friend. Her best friend this week, at least—they were always fighting, it seemed, and then the next week they acted like nothing ever happened. Marina had trouble keeping up.

"Are you really going to eat all of that?" said Annabelle to Marina as she slid into her seat. Marina froze, suddenly self-conscious of her overflowing tray.

"I'm just really hungry," she said as Lulu and Roxy sat down too.

"I would throw up if I ate that much," said Annabelle, wrinkling her nose. "I haven't eaten carbs in, like, two years. I wish I could be like Lulu." She glanced over at Marina's full tray again, her lips pursing. "She's the only person I know who can eat whatever she wants without looking like a fat pig."

Lulu smirked and shrugged breezily as she took another bite of her sandwich, and Marina knew her cheeks were flaming. Annabelle might as well have just said out loud that Lulu was the only one at the table capable of eating that way and still looking good. Her macaroni salad turned to clay in her mouth. For a moment, it seemed as though everyone was staring at her and her tray and her mouth, currently full of macaroni. Then the moment passed, and Roxy started talking about something that happened in gymnastics, and the awkwardness passed. Marina set her fork down, trying to act natural. If she didn't act embarrassed there was no reason for anyone else to realize how uncomfortable Annabelle had made her.

Marina snuck a glance at Annabelle, to see if the snarky look was still on her face, but she'd turned to whisper something to Victoria, who just looked bored. Not bored like Marina would look, though—bored like a queen, regal and disdainful. Marina brushed a frizzy part of her hair out of her eyes and tried to adopt the same expression. She pushed around the rest of her macaroni until the end of lunch. Her stomach was grumbling but she couldn't quite bring herself to keep eating. She still felt like everyone was watching her, and she was aware of her body in a way that made even shifting at the table embarrassing. She felt so self-conscious, like a whale sitting in her plaid skirt and her button-up shirt, the buttons straining just a little across the middle. Finally, lunch was over and Marina got up with the rest of the group. She dumped her full tray in the wastebasket, a twinge of guilt in her aching stomach. There was always enough food at her house, so it wasn't like she'd ever gone hungry, but she still felt bad wasting so much.

Just don't get so much next time, thought Marina. *Then you won't have to look like a pig, and you won't have to throw it away.* Doing her best to ignore her mostly-empty tummy, Marina trailed behind Lulu and the rest of the girls as they headed back to class.

Chapter Four

By the time she changed for dance practice, Marina was so hungry she thought she might pass out right there onstage. She went through the motions hollowly, trying to ignore the ache in her stomach, but she wasn't used to going so long without food. During a break she found an old Pop-Tart in her bag and scarfed it, and after that she felt much better, albeit giggly from the sugar. Still, pirouette drills seemed even more difficult than usual; she had trouble focusing enough to find her rhythm, and tried to stay behind Annabelle, who was the pirouette professional out of the entire group.

Her mouth might always have that pinched look to it, but there was no denying that her bony body with her perfect bun almost never made a mistake.

"Watch it," said Lulu as Marina stumbled a step during a drill. "I almost just stepped on you."

"I'm sorry," sighed Marina, wiping sweat from her brow. "I'm just really tired today."

Finally, practice was over, and Ms. Bennett called them all to the front of the dance room. Marina held the barre with one hand, planning what she would eat for dinner. They were serving double-smoked salmon with horseradish cream in the dining hall tonight, one of her favorite dishes here. On top of that, the chefs had gotten a little crazy and made eight different varieties of sugar cookies, and right now Marina would happily sample each of them. Twice. Marina rolled her ankles, leaning from one leg to the other and fanning herself with one hand.

"Just a reminder, we will be having tryouts for positions in the showcase here pretty soon," said Ms. Bennett. She was a portly, stately woman with dark hair streaked with gray that was perpetually slicked into a ballet bun. "In six weeks or so we'll hold tryouts, and all of you except the seniors will learn the same combination so we can assess everyone's participation in the showcase in May. So please be prepared to stay for late practices from then on up until the showcase. We'll all have a lot to work on."

Marina was almost too hungry to feel the familiar swoop of nerves in her tummy at the thought of auditioning. The worst part is that the seniors all got to sit in on the auditions and watch all the younger girls perform the number. Marina heard that before she was a senior Annabelle somehow edged out one of the current seniors for a spot she wanted. There were rumors of a broken ankle, but Marina wasn't sure any of it was true. This year, though, Annabelle would be one of the seniors watching Marina audition, and that was just terrifying. The rest of the end of practice speech went right through Marina—she could hear Ms. Bennett talking, and she tried to pay attention, but really all she was thinking of was garlic-braised potatoes. When she finally closed the practice, Marina was the first one in line in the rush back to the locker room, and she grabbed her bag and her inhaler and headed right back out again. She'd sit in the dining hall in her warm-ups and her leotard, she didn't care—she just needed to eat.

Marina checked in with the dorm head in the dining hall, then Marina grabbed a tray and prepared to load it with every single dessert offered that night. There was a German chocolate-bourbon cake, a raspberry cheesecake she'd been dying to try, not to mention white-chocolate key lime pie, plus all the sugar cookies, of course. Marina grabbed one of each dessert, and then she heard the voices of the dance team behind her. She'd run off so fast after practice that she'd beaten them all to dinner. Marina hastily replaced half of her desserts and took a single serving of the salmon dish. She sat down next to a few girls in her year and started eating; instantly she felt better, more alert and chatty. She continued shoving bites of salmon in her mouth as the dance team, Roxy, Lulu, and a few other roommates of dance and gymnastics team girls sat down around her.

"I'm so nervous for the showcase auditions," said Lulu, nibbling daintily on a bread roll. "I mean, is everyone really going to be watching us?"

"Yeah," Marina spoke up from the other end of the table. "They all sit at the front of the room, typically."

"So nerve-wracking."

"Stop complaining," said Annabelle, setting her tray down across from Marina. "It's not that bad."

"Easy for you to say, you're a senior," grumbled Lulu.

"I'm already bored of this conversation and I just sat down," said Victoria, tossing her hair to the side as she claimed a seat next to Annabelle.

"Don't be dramatic, Victoria," said Annabelle.

"Let's talk about something fun," said Victoria, sneaking a sideways glance across the table. "Let's talk about how we're all going to an off-campus party soon."

"What?" said Lulu.

"A party. My friend has people over pretty much every weekend at her parent's house in Beverly Hills. We can all go sometime."

"I can't go this weekend," said Lulu. "My parents are coming to visit."

"Next weekend?" Victoria said.

"The weekend after next works best for me," said Annabelle, flipping through her planner.

"That's fine for me, too," Marina piped in. Lulu glanced at her but the rest of the girls just kept talking, caught up in the potential excitement of going to a party.

Marina took another bite of pudding, listening to them gossip. She'd need a pass to be out late on Friday, but her mom would sign it for her. Marina knew she wanted her to make friends, and be a part of the group the way her mom was when she went here. Her mom had been dance team captain for two years. Marina had seen the pictures a thousand times of her dancing at the point position in countless showcases, endless recitals. She had a grace and poise that Marina knew she could never hope to replicate—she didn't have the length in leg or arm that her mother had, or the face that looked like it'd been sculpted from clay by an artist, but Marina would do the most she could with what she had. Marina glanced down at her Michael Kors watch; it was rose gold and inlaid with the brightest pink she could find. It was getting late and she still had homework to do that she'd been putting off.

"I gotta go," said Marina. "See you guys tomorrow."

Roxy waved, but the rest barely seemed to notice when Marina got up and left the table, carrying her now-empty tray. She waved at one of the chefs as she moved toward the trash can.

"Thank you for making the cheesecake," said Marina, smiling. "It was delicious."

"Certainly, miss. We're glad you enjoyed it."

"If you wanted to make those caramel-pecan tarts again next week, I wouldn't mind that," said Marina, even though she knew she shouldn't. She was so full from dinner and all the desserts she'd eaten that she could burst, and she needed to start her diet as soon as possible to get ready for showcase auditions. Still, a treat just sounded *so good.*

Marina waved goodbye to the chef and walked out the double doors of the dining commons. She needed a shower, badly, and then she needed to get her butt to the library and study so she wouldn't be the only one who didn't know what was going on in this English project of hers. Poetry definitely wasn't her strong point. It was just confusing. Trying to guess what someone meant to say through imagery was so inefficient. *Why not just say what you mean?* Marina thought. *Seems like it would've saved everyone a lot of time and effort.*

Marina hopped into the shower, rinsing her thick curls and then doing her best to smooth them down again as she dressed in sweats and a Beverly Hills Preparatory Academy sweatshirt, complete with the scarlet and gold crest. She grabbed her books and backpack and breezed through her and Lulu's common room. Marina opened the door and paused as she heard voices in the hallway.

"Yeah, you can borrow my blue dress if you want. It might be a little short on you but I'm sure it will still work."

"Okay, perfect. Nora took my favorite one and I never got it back. Still not sure what that's about, but I promise not to do that to you."

Marina poked her head around the door and waved at the group. Lulu was talking to Lauren, from the gymnastics team, and her twin Sasha. Roxy stood there too, twisting her red hair around her fingers.

"Hey, guys! I'm just heading to the library. What are you all talking about?"

"Nothing," said Lulu, but Lauren poked her head around.

"Just outfits in case we decide to go to Victoria's friend's party in a couple weeks."

"Oh, nice," said Marina. "I hadn't even thought about that. I have a ton of outfits, though, and dresses that we picked up in Barcelona last summer if anyone wants to borrow anything from me."

Lauren opened her mouth, but before she could say anything Lulu cut in.

"I don't think any of us would really fit into your clothes, Marina."

Marina gripped her notebook a little more tightly as her stomach sank, but she refused to really acknowledge what Lulu was saying.

"What do you mean? Some stuff might not fit perfectly, sure, but it's one night at a party so . . . does it really matter?"

"It will all be too big for us," said Lulu bitingly. "Especially in the hips, let's say. And I don't really want you taking anything of mine and stretching it out, either."

There was a moment of total quiet in the hallway, interrupted only by the opening and closing doors and murmurs of other conversations that passed by Marina. Her eyes welled with tears. She thought she'd come so far with Lulu. She'd thought they were almost friends. Lauren and Sasha just stood there. Roxy's face was bright red, but she bit her lip and stayed quiet. Marina didn't know what to do, so she just stood there like an idiot gripping her notebook like a life raft.

"Well, we're going to go to bed," said Lauren finally, with a pointed look at Sasha and Roxy. "See you tomorrow."

Then all three of them scurried off, darting glances back at Lulu and Marina and whispering until they turned a corner and were gone.

"I'm going to bed, too," said Lulu, and then she nudged her way past Marina and went into their dorm, the front door clicking shut behind her. Marina stood in the hallway, and finally the tears escaped her eyes as she silently choked, trying not to cry. She turned blindly, walking toward the library. As she walked, she felt the material of her sweatpants rubbing against the backs of her hips, and the sensation filled her with embarrassment. *How many other girls had been thinking what Lulu had said out loud?* With every step, Marina felt the tears fall and she wished more than anything that she could go somewhere, anywhere, and hide from the entire world.

Chapter Five

Marina walked toward the entrance to the Clara Barton Library, one of Beverly Hills Prep's smallest and most private of all the libraries on campus. When she burst through the doors, the librarian at the oak front desk was the only other person she saw in the room. Wiping her eyes, Marina found her booth and sat down inside it, finally away from the crowds in the hallways. She grabbed her inhaler and breathed in deeply, trying to calm down. Finally, she was hiccupping and not sobbing. Marina pulled out her backpack and got her laptop; she still had an hour or so before lights out. It would be best if she just forgot what Lulu said and got to work on her homework.

But as she opened her laptop, she found herself clicking on her photo albums instead of her English homework. There were old screenshots of her mom, pictures she'd scanned for a photography project last year. There were pictures of her mother in pink leotards, Marina's age, en pointe on stage, dancing as a prima ballerina. Marina flicked through them one by one, taking in her posture, her flawless technique, even in the stillness of a photograph. Mostly, though, she saw her tiny waist, her long, slim legs, and her perfect arms. Marina wanted to look just like her, and although people said they had the same smile and the same nose, Marina wanted all the rest.

I can have that, she thought. *I can have it—I just have to work for it. I have to want it bad enough.*

Marina's mind went back to the lunch table, went back to Annabelle's snide comments and Lulu's cruel words in the hallway. Maybe she didn't deserve it, that was true, but Marina did want her body to be better than it was. Maybe this was just a sign that she needed to commit to it. She checked her watch; lights out was in fifteen minutes. Sighing, Marina grabbed her backpack and stuffed her laptop inside, swinging it onto her back as she headed back to her room. She hoped Lulu was sleeping. The last thing she needed was to see her face again tonight.

As she walked down the hallway toward her room, Roxy's freckled face appeared across from her.

"Hey, Marina," she said, her eyes full of apologies. "Want to grab a snack before the dining hall closes?"

Marina looked at her, remembered the way she'd just stood there and stared when Lulu said what she had. She would love to eat an entire batch of brownies right now, too, but that was also a terrible idea. She wanted to go with Roxy, she really did. But if she went she'd eat a snack, and somehow she couldn't shake off the pity she saw now in Roxy's eyes.

"No, thanks," said Marina, and she walked into her dorm and shut the door firmly behind her.

For the next few days, Marina clung to her diet with the ferocity of a lion—if a lion were trying to lose twenty-five pounds, which Marina doubted was ever an issue for a lion. She got used to choosing the apple and walnut salad with no dressing instead of the Havarti cheesesteak sandwiches on handmade sourdough bread, and she never took dessert. Her trays were almost as empty as Annabelle's, but not quite. It seemed like she could never quite stop thinking about food; the best she could do was distract herself for a while, but that was a deal Marina was willing to take for pounds lost. She weighed herself every morning, knowing that it would take time for the numbers to go down, but also just to make sure that they at least weren't going up. She cheated a little more toward the end of the week, scarfing a chewy chocolate and coconut granola bar at the end of dance practice during a particularly weak moment. But other than that, she was good.

"I'm dieting again," she told her mother over the phone on Sunday afternoon, as she tried to distract herself from the thought of food with the homework she'd put off another day. "Trying to get down to a goal weight before the auditions for showcase spots."

"Sounds like a good plan to me, honey," said her mother in her husky voice, still rich with the Spanish accent she'd never quite lost. "Just don't worry about it too much. You don't need to be stick thin to be a wonderful dancer."

"Easy for you to say," said Marina, irritable with hunger. "You're the best dancer I've ever seen."

Her mom laughed, and Marina heard the gurgle of her little brother over the line. She wished she was there, helping her mom with dinner, instead of hungry and alone at school. She'd been avoiding Lulu for days. Lulu didn't seem too concerned. But, she did have the grace to at least seem surprised when she came into the common room and Marina's only response was to look up and blink, and then go back to her book instead of setting it down and trying to chat like she normally did.

"I was good, honey, but all I cared about was dancing. It was what I lived for, at least until I met your father and had you and your brothers and sisters."

"Is that bad?"

"No, not necessarily. It taught me strength, and discipline."

Marina wished she had more of both of those things. Her mom still had gnarled and twisted bones in her feet from years of dance work. Marina could barely go an hour without a pudding cup.

"I gotta finish this homework up, Mama," said Marina. "I'll call you tomorrow, okay?"

"Okay, honey. Talk to you soon."

Marina pressed END and flopped back down on her comforter. She wanted angel food cake. She wanted a whole pie, all to herself. Sighing, she pushed herself up. She needed to get a granola bar and go to the dance room for a workout.

Marina aced her World History quiz on Monday, largely because she'd been trying to distract herself all weekend by actually studying and avoiding Lulu and the rest of the girls. She kept her head down on Tuesday when Annabelle and Victoria passed by, and she flattened herself against the wall when she heard Lulu's voice after lunch. But by Friday, she was ready to make up with Lulu just because she was so bored of keeping to herself. The incident in the hallway felt less terrible in her mind since it had been a few days, and she'd gotten close to a week of good dieting in. She felt more in control now that she was on the right track, even though she was tired of spinach. At lunch, she chose an iceberg lettuce salad with lemon juice and cashews, and it was all she ate until dance practice.

Marina walked into the dance annex, and down the tiled hallway that always smelled of chalk and disinfectant, a comforting smell she'd grown used to.

She always forgot about this side effect of dieting, but she did like the way she felt when she danced and she wasn't stuffed with muffins or a milkshake. Sometimes all that happened was her stomach growled the whole time, loudly, but sometimes she forgot about how hungry she was, and she just danced. No thoughts, no distracting worry about whether or not anyone had seen her mess up that last step. She just listened to the beat of the music, the rise and fall of Ms. Bennett's voice as she counted through the notes, and somehow her body knew exactly what to do. She was normally a self-conscious dancer, half a beat behind because she was afraid to do the wrong move before everyone else. But not tonight—not when she felt like this, like her feet were made from feathers and wings.

When Ms. Bennett called for the end of practice and the music stopped, she was surprised. She hadn't been watching the clock or thinking about dinner or anything. The number was calming to her, and she'd been focused on the choreography. Ms. Bennett liked to recycle certain eight counts from her favorite pieces, and Marina had a hunch she was going to do that with the piece she would prepare for the showcase auditions.

"Good work, today," said Ms. Bennett. "I saw a lot of potential out there, and I'm paying close attention. Even for you seniors with a guaranteed part in the showcase, you could get more or less time depending on the effort I see you putting in in the next few months."

Marina saw a few seniors glance at each other anxiously. Annabelle stood with her pointed nose straight in the air, as usual.

"Marina," said Ms. Bennett, and Marina's eyebrows raised. *What had she done now?* She looked down. Her leotard was pink, same as everyone else. One day she'd worn the black by accident and everyone had laughed as soon as she walked into the dance room.

"You did well today," said Ms. Bennett. "Really well. I think a few of you could stand to learn a few things from her discipline. She's obviously been practicing."

Marina stood up a little straighter as a few girls

glanced her way. Some of the seniors looked at her in a way she'd never seen before; just for a moment, they looked at her like she was their competition. Annabelle's gaze flicked over her, a cool assessment, like Marina was some kind of specimen she was forced to examine. Then the moment was gone, and everyone was talking, heading to the locker room to change out of their leotards and tights before dinner. Ms. Bennett smiled at Marina as she walked out, and Marina grinned at her. She practically danced down the hallway to the locker room. She hadn't felt this light in a long time.

In the locker room, Marina grabbed her hot pink gym bag and scooted into the corner, facing the wall, the way she always changed. The other girls chattered while they came back and forth from the shower to the lockers in towels or stripped down to change into sweats. Lulu with her tiny, perfectly curved body never seemed to want to put clothes back on at all and would stand and talk in just her sports bra and shorts. Annabelle was a little more modest, but she still stood in the middle of the room and changed without hesitation. No one seemed to feel the way Marina did, like she would die if anyone saw her without at least a leotard on. Even tonight, feeling as confident as she did after that practice, she couldn't bring herself to face away from the wall as she shimmied off her tights and yanked sweats back on as quickly as she could.

"Marina, can I borrow a hair tie? Mine just broke."

Lulu stood behind Marina, so close she wanted to jump when she heard her voice. Marina hadn't managed to pull her top on yet, so she stood in her sports bra and sweats.

"Sure thing," she said, trying to keep her voice light, but she didn't like having Lulu so close when she didn't have a shirt on. What if she saw her bare tummy? Marina awkwardly tugged the hair tie off her own wrist and reached sideways toward Lulu while trying to pull her shirt over herself at the same time. As soon as Lulu's fingers touched hers she pulled away and wiggled into her shirt, her cheeks flaming. Lulu still stood behind her, almost smirking, amused at Marina's obvious discomfort.

"Thanks," she said, flashing a smile that didn't reach her eyes, and then Annabelle turned, grabbing her own bag on the way out the door. Marina let out a long breath. She wanted to cry and wasn't entirely sure why.

At dinner Marina went with the broiled skinless chicken breast and roasted asparagus, although she did allow herself a tiny slice of stuffed angel food cake because Ms. Bennett had noticed her losing weight. She wasn't a better dancer this week than she'd been all year; no, her instructor had noticed that Marina was on the right track. The only time she danced the way she did tonight was when she was feeling confident, and the only time she really felt confident was when she was dieting. Still . . . *One more bite of the cake wasn't*

going to set me back that far, she thought. *Just one more bite and I'll throw it away.*

"So are we going to this party tomorrow or what?" said Annabelle, sliding into a seat next to Victoria, who twirled broccoli on her fork and looked bored.

"What about tonight?"

"I can't tonight," snapped Annabelle to Victoria. "You know that. I have to wait for my mom to fax the release over and she won't be back from the resort until tomorrow."

"You said this weekend worked for you."

"It does, just not tonight. It's Friday. It isn't technically the weekend yet."

"Sounds like your own problem," said Victoria breezily, in a voice like poisoned honey. Annabelle's face turned a mottled shade of almost purple that Marina had never seen before. "I'm ready to go out," Victoria continued. "There's nothing else to do. I'll call a car for us and everyone who has a release can come with."

Marina stuffed cake into her mouth almost without

realizing what she was doing, she was so uncomfortable. Victoria could be so mean. She looked at Annabelle's narrowed eyes and her mouth, pressed into the thinnest line imaginable, and she was almost afraid to go.

"I'll go," said Roxy. "Sorry, Annabelle, but tonight works for me—I failed an algebra test and I really don't want to think about it."

"Maybe you should stay in and study if you failed," snapped Annabelle, but Roxy just rolled her eyes. Vivienne, with her dark hair and dimples, was nowhere to be seen at the table, so Marina couldn't gauge her reaction. She'd gone to the initiation of the new girls from the field hockey and gymnastics team a few weeks ago, because Lulu had gone to see Roxy, and Vivienne had disappeared like halfway through it. So did Marina, though—Lulu left to talk to Roxy and Marina hadn't wanted to stand in the dark by herself.

"I'll go, too," said Marina. "I mean, if there's room in the car. My mom sent the release over a few days ago."

It was true—Marina was so afraid of something happening to her like what had just happened to Annabelle that she'd had her mom sign the form and email it over the day after anyone had even brought up the possibility of going out.

Victoria looked her over briefly, and all Marina could think was that she hoped she didn't have cake on her face. Victoria shrugged. "Sure."

"Me, too," said Lulu. "It sounds like fun."

"Perfect. If anyone else adds on just text me so I can call another car."

"You want to pay for two cars?"

Victoria laughed out loud, her blond hair slipping over her shoulder like gold satin. "I don't think Daddy will mind. Anyway, let's be ready to get out of here in about an hour. No one be late. I want to leave on time."

And with that, Victoria got up from the table like a queen rising from her throne, tossed her bare tray to the side, and swept out of the dining hall. Annabelle stormed out after her, her mousy hair flying in a cloud behind her. For a moment, the table was silent.

"So, what are you guys going to wear?" said Roxy.

Chapter Six

"Lulu, are you ready yet? You know Victoria will leave without us if we aren't ready."

Marina tapped her foot impatiently. She would never normally yell at Lulu, but she didn't want them to be left behind. Taking advantage of Lulu's slowness, Marina ran back into her room to check her outfit in the mirror one more time.

She was wearing a pink dress, of course—dark pink, almost red, and it was tight and strapless, perfect for a fancy house party. She'd bought it in Barcelona, but as soon as her dad saw her trying to wear it to dinner he'd made her go change. The black heels she was wearing were just low enough so that she knew she wouldn't fall over; the last thing she needed was everyone thinking she was immature because she couldn't walk in heels. Her hair was hastily curled and thrown up into a loose up-do with tendrils raining down, and her makeup was shimmery and smoky, her eyes huge with nerves. Heart pounding, Marina smoothed down the sleek material of her dress. She was going out with the most popular girls in school. Marina grabbed her inhaler from the dresser, breathing in deeply. *It's going to be fine,* she told herself. *Relax. If they see you're nervous they won't think you belong, but you do.* Thank God she'd been dieting. If she felt fat, Marina knew she would never have the courage to go.

"Marina, let's go! I'm ready!"

Now she was the one who looked late. Sighing, Marina grabbed her purse and a full-length jacket that covered her nearly to her ankles. The dorm head would never let her out the door if she saw what she was really wearing. The girls were allowed to leave, with their passes, but that didn't mean they were allowed to leave in short dresses and fake eyelashes. But Marina ran to the door anyway, ducking her head in case there was someone patrolling the halls who would see her makeup.

Lulu's dress was light blue, and not as tight as Marina's, but shorter. Marina felt better seeing that—she wasn't the only one trying to look older than she was. They hurried down the hallway, awkward in heels, Lulu's hair slipping out of its bobby pins. Marina started to giggle senselessly, sliding as the carpeted floor met hardwood, and Lulu shot her a grin over the back of her shoulder. They had to go out of their dormitory and into the night air briefly to reach the Meadows dormitory, where Victoria and mostly other seniors lived. Lulu peeked through the glass at the top of the entrance, checking to see if the faculty resident or the dorm head were there, but all they saw was an older woman asleep at the desk, snoring. Tiptoeing, the girls snuck past her and then sprinted for Victoria's room at the end of the hall.

She opened the door right as they arrived, breathless. Roxy and a few other girls were in tow behind her, and when Marina got a full look at Victoria she wished for her inhaler again. She was in all black, sleek and simple, her hair done in waves that flowed down her back. Marina felt like an elf next to Victoria's long legs. Her makeup was smudged at the corners, accentuating her ice blue eyes. Victoria hadn't even bothered to put a coat on like the rest of the girls; Marina admired her courage. She didn't think she'd survive a resident seeing her in her pink dress.

"Let's go," Victoria said, and everyone filed in behind her, whispering and giggling and trying not to be too loud. Marina held her breath, afraid to even speak until they'd gotten out of the dorm and into the parking lot.

"Let me see your dress, Marina," said Roxy, pulling at her coat, and Marina opened it shyly so the pink shone through.

"I love that color. I can never pull off jewel tones, but they look so good against your skin."

"Thanks," said Marina, genuinely grateful, and then a black Escalade pulled up to the curb. Victoria climbed in, followed by Marina and a few others, and the rest of the group followed suit in the second car.

"Play Beyoncé," squealed Roxy in the backseat, but Victoria shook her head, ordering the driver to put on something by an artist Marina didn't recognize, and the driver nodded toward her, turning the knob as a song began to blare that Marina hadn't heard before. She still listened to her Jessica Simpson CD that she'd had since the sixth grade.

"Okay," said Lulu as the car pulled away from the curb. "Does anyone want some soda before we get there? I brought energy drinks, you know, those ones that are practically banned for having so much caffeine."

"I want one," said Roxy, taking a swig from a neon can. "I'm exhausted from this week. But sometimes all the sugar makes me queasy."

"If you throw up, I'm leaving you there," said Victoria.

"Have some, Marina," ordered Lulu. "You look tired."

Marina laughed, shaking her head, and grabbed an energy drink. She wasn't normally a big caffeine drinker, but she was a little tired and she wanted to be bright and alert so she could chat with everyone at the party.

"I can't wait to dance all night," said Lulu, taking another sip of her energy drink. "There are going to be guys there, right?"

"Yeah, of course," said Victoria.

"Good. I'm in the market for a new boyfriend."

Marina chewed on her lip; she knew in the back of her mind this wasn't an all-girl party, they weren't in the fifth grade anymore, but she was nervous all over again at the thought of boys being there.

"Turn the music up," said Victoria to the driver. "I can't listen to freshmen gossip anymore." As people always seemed to, he obeyed her.

Marina took another sip of her energy drink, the street lights shining into the car and illuminating everyone's face for seconds at a time—Lulu's sly grin, Roxy's open-mouthed laugh, Victoria's perfect sneer. Marina took another drink and let her jacket slide to the floor. She wasn't cold, and somehow she wasn't afraid that the other girls would see how the material of her dress looked against her hips. Her heart started to pound even faster as the caffeine and sugar went to her head, and Marina smiled.

The trip seemed to pass in seconds, and then they were there at the curb in front of the house, which was located in a gated community. Marina's stomach clutched with nerves again, briefly, but she clambered out with everyone else as another sleek car pulled up behind them. Victoria led the group to the front of the line, past everyone else waiting, and Marina watched each person's eyes light on her as she passed. Some watched Marina, though, too, and she saw a couple boys who looked a few years older than her looking at her admiringly. Marina wiggled her dress down a few inches, then stopped as the person at the door glared at her. *Did they really have a line and a bouncer for a house party?* It did look more like a resort than a house— Marina could see what looked like three floors, plus a pool in the backyard. She tried smiling through her nervousness.

There were two guys at the door controlling who came inside—tall, muscular men looking Victoria over appreciatively as she was chatting with them. Tilting her head so her hair cascaded over her shoulder, Victoria laughed at something one of them said, reaching forward to touch his arm. Marina tried to mimic her confidence, pulling out her phone and attempting to seem impatient. It only took a few more seconds, though, and then one of the guys was ushering their entire group inside and through the double front doors. All it had taken was Victoria's smile.

Marina tried to act casual and not like a star-struck teenager, but the inside of the house was completely overwhelming. Blue and green lights flashed from the

DJ stand that was raised on a platform in the foyer, and music was pounding in time with the lights. People were dancing on a makeshift dance floor in the enormous living room, and the winding staircase showed people chatting and walking along the balconies. There were coconut and island-style decorations everywhere, like they were somewhere on a beach in the middle of the Pacific. In the background, Marina heard splashing and shrieks as someone, she guessed, dove into the pool. Marina glanced down, tripping slightly in the dark.

"I've met those two bouncers a few times," said Victoria, turning to talk to the group and raising her voice over the music. "Nice guys. I need to find my friend—she's here somewhere. Follow me."

They walked into the house, through the foyer and past the living room until they were in the kitchen, and then they were outside on the patio, the bright blue underwater pool lights glowing in the dark.

Marina walked to the edge of the pool, which had a waterfall and several separate Jacuzzi tubs along the sides. Everyone was milling around the pool and along the back patio, which seemed to go on forever. Marina thought she saw a few of the boys who'd been looking at her outside in the flash of the lights. Lulu and Roxy were already grabbing fruity virgin daiquiris at the makeshift bar, and Victoria was hugging her friend, having located her by the pool. The DJ started a new song and Marina swayed to the music. Before she knew what was happening she was swinging her hips and tossing her hair as the beat moved through her, bobby pins flying through the air as her curls tumbled down. Then Lulu was there, then Roxy, and another girl she didn't know, and they were all dancing together, squealing as Roxy dipped her head and spilled half her drink everywhere. Marina edged out of the group, Lulu coming with her, and headed toward the Hawaiian-style bar.

"What can I get you ladies?" asked the bartender, his biceps bulging against his sleeves.

"Can we get a couple of those pineapple daiquiris?" said Lulu. "Is that fine with you, Marina?"

"Yeah, that sounds good," said Marina. "These are virgin, right?"

"I'm not trying to get arrested tonight, miss," chuckled the bartender. "Yes, all the drinks are alcohol-free."

"Thanks," said Marina, grinning. She was starting to feel a little sick from all the sugar in the energy drinks, but the fruity daiquiris looked so cute with their little umbrella hats. She watched him mix the two drinks, plopping strawberries into both their cups.

"Let's go dance over there on the patio," said Lulu over the music. "I want to dance with someone besides all these girls."

"Okay," said Marina, and the two walked together down the stairs to the lower patio. They stepped into the throng of people and dancing bodies, trying to avoid having drinks splashed on them as people laughed and talked and danced. Marina turned around somewhere in the middle of the dance floor, awkwardly pushing her way between a group of people, and saw Lulu dancing with a boy in a dark grey shirt a few feet away. Marina paused, uncertain now in the crowd, standing alone.

"Hey," she heard someone shout in her ear, and she spun to find one of the smiling boys from outside. He didn't look a lot older than she was, and as far as she could tell in the darkness he had an easy smile. "What are you drinking?" he asked.

Before she could respond someone bumped into Marina from behind and she lurched forward, grabbing the stranger's shoulders. He was strong and his shoulders were firm, and she saw the flash of his smile in the lights.

"A pineapple daiquiri," she said. "Want a sip?"

"I'm good, thanks, sweetheart."

"No problem." Marina smiled at him as she took another sip, trying to copy the way Lulu managed to look sweet and dangerous at the same time.

"I'm Rob," he said, practically shouting into her ear. "What's your name?"

Should she come up with a fake one? Too late to

do that now. The only name she could think of was her own.

"Marina," she half-shouted back, and then she slid her hands back up to his shoulders, still clutching her drink in one hand, sipping it as she danced. Marina leaned closer to him, so close her cheek was almost pressed to his; he smelled like cologne and something spicy, and she didn't mind the combination at all.

Marina closed her eyes and let him move her, holding her fingertips and spinning her around. She paused, unsure, but his motion guided her own and soon she was dancing again, one hand in the air as the music blasted, the other holding her drink. In the dark, with a stranger, in a huge group of people, Marina felt completely free. She sipped from her straw and got only air. She needed another drink. She also really, really needed to pee.

"I'll be right back," she shouted at Rob, motioning toward the house. He nodded, waving her on, and she started to shove her way through the crowd as best she could. Everyone on the patio seemed to have multiplied. *How long had she been dancing with Rob? It hadn't felt like more than a few minutes.*

She walked down a marble hallway until she saw a line of girls already waiting for the bathroom. Marina got in line, shifting from foot to foot as she watched girls in dresses even tighter than hers walk out. The line took forever, and by the time Marina got into the bathroom she would have cut herself out of the stupid tight dress just so she could pee. Sighing with relief, she yanked it back down over her hips again. She was so sweaty that it kept getting stuck. She washed her hands in the granite sink and walked out carefully, trying to avoid the water on the floor that was just waiting for her to slip in it. Outside again, she got a glimpse of who she thought was Rob, his back to her; she recognized the color of his shirt and his hair, and when he turned and smiled she knew it was him.

"Rob!" said Marina, shoving through the crowd, and he turned at his name. He was holding a drink with an umbrella in it, white instead of yellow.

"Hey again," he said, smiling at her as she

approached him and the group of people he was standing with. It looked like a few other guys around his age, one with blond hair and one who looked ready to leave. "I got you a piña colada. Is that okay?"

"Virgin, right?"

"Yeah, of course," he said.

"Wow, thanks," said Marina, accepting the glass from his hand. She beamed at him, delighted that he'd been thinking of her. He was still looking at her, so she sipped it and smiled so he'd know she appreciated it.

"So, do you wanna dance?" said Marina.

"Sure thing, honey."

"Okay."

Marina happily sipped her drink, moving a little to the music as Rob started chatting with his friends. The one who looked impatient was practically glaring at Marina. He leaned forward and said something to Rob, who just rolled his eyes and said something back about him being jealous. He grabbed Marina's hand, and she let herself be tugged back onto the patio where people were dancing.

"What was he saying?" she asked as they moved back into the center of the makeshift floor again.

"Oh, him? Nothing. He just wants to go home because he doesn't see any girls on the dance floor that he likes."

"But you do, right?" said Marina, smiling as Rob turned to face her and their hips began to sway in tandem.

"Sure do," he said appreciatively, running his hands down her sides. "I like a girl with plenty of meat on her bones. You've sure got some curves on you."

Marina's heart nearly stopped.

"What did you just say?"

He blinked at her, at least that's what she thought he did—the darkness made it sort of hard to tell. She must have misheard him.

"I said I like a girl with a little meat on her bones. I didn't mean it in a bad way or anything—"

Marina stared at him, and then she shoved him away, spilling half her drink on his shirt in the process.

"Hey! Hey, I said I didn't mean it in a bad way!"

"You don't just say something like that to some-body!" Marina shouted back over her shoulder.

What a jerk, thought Marina. She kept walking away from him, fighting her way through the crowd on the floor. It was time to find her friends, anyway. The sugar from those drinks must be starting to hit because she felt queasy, or maybe it was just the way he'd made her feel.

She didn't care in what way he'd meant the comment. All she knew was that she had to get out of here and get out of this stupid dress that was too tight before she started crying in front of the entire party.

Chapter Seven

Marina barely remembered the drive back to Beverly Hills Prep. She sat in the seat next to Roxy and tried to act interested in the gossip the rest of the girls were chattering about, but her heart wasn't in it. Victoria sat in the front seat and sighed impatiently every time they hit a red light. Marina leaned against the window, her foot tapping wildly—she was still totally hyped from the sugar rush.

The next thing she knew, they were back at the school, pulling into the resident parking lot. The group tiptoed quietly back to the dormitories. As long as they were present in their rooms at seven in the morning on Saturday, they didn't need to check in with anyone now, which Marina was thankful for.

"You go ahead back to our dorm," said Lulu to Marina once they'd let themselves into their dormitory. "I'm going to walk Roxy back to her room."

"Sounds good," mumbled Marina. Victoria was nowhere to be found. She'd probably just went straight back to her own dormitory. Marina dropped her dorm key twice, her hands shaking, before she fit it to the lock and let herself inside. She immediately dropped her coat on the floor and unlocked her phone, but no one had texted her. Walking into her room, Marina struggled to unzip her dress's zipper—finally, she heard a tear and it came off, dropping to the floor. Marina left it there and turned the shower on. She could still smell Rob's cologne on her, and she just wanted to erase all memory of him. *Why was she still thinking about it? What did it even matter?*

The hot water ran over her body and Marina hugged herself, arms wrapped around her middle, but she felt no comfort. She started to cry, her tears mingling with the hot water. She'd thought he was so sweet. She wanted him to see her the way boys looked at Victoria, not like another chubby girl who should be grateful to get a free drink from him. All of a sudden, Marina couldn't bear to look at her body for another second. She turned the water off and grabbed a towel, wrapping herself up tight from her knees to her shoulders. Then she climbed into bed, towel and all, and curled up into a ball under the sheets. Her feet ached, and she had a headache from the noise and the music. Tonight had started off so perfectly, and then everything had gone wrong. All she wanted to do was forget it had ever happened, but she didn't think she could. She'd never be able to erase the feeling of his hands on her as he insulted her, and she hated him for that.

Marina woke up the next morning certain that there was a tiny construction worker in her brain who was insistent on hammering her eyes open from the inside. Too much sugar always gave her a headache.

Wait. What time was it? The dorm head was doing check-in at seven. Just like that, Marina heard a knock at the door.

"Lulu? Marina? It's time for Saturday check-in."

"Oh, no," whispered Marina. They'd gotten back too late last night that she'd totally forgotten. Marina leapt frantically from the bed, ignoring her still-aching feet to pull on sweatpants from the floor and a shirt from the back of her desk chair. The living area was fairly neat, but Marina's room was a wreck. Was Lulu even here? As she thought it, Marina's bedroom door swung open. Lulu stood outside it, hair standing straight up on one side. She was still in last night's dress.

"What are we going to do?" she hissed at Marina as another knock came at the door.

"Just open it. We'll get written up but we don't have any checks yet that we've failed; we'll be fine. But go change out of your dress."

Lulu sprinted across the living room to her bedroom, pulling her dress over her head as she went. Marina walked to the door and opened it to the dorm head standing outside. She was a senior student with huge glasses and stick straight blond hair whose face seemed to be set in a perpetual expression of annoyance.

"Good morning," said Marina sweetly.

"Why aren't you in uniform?"

"Oh, sorry." Marina smoothed down her T-shirt. "I just overslept."

Marina saw the dorm head's gaze sweep over her, taking in her hair—loose curls in a riot around her face—and the smudged makeup she hadn't quite removed completely.

"So, come in," said Marina as Lulu ran out of her room in pajamas. "I know you have to do your inspection."

"I'm going to write up both of you for being out of uniform."

"On a Saturday? Really?" Lulu rolled her eyes.

"You're both underclassmen. You know the rules."

Marina didn't care about being written up for a uniform violation as long as no one found out how late they had come in last night. Then they'd really be in trouble. She and Lulu stood and watched the dorm head poke around their dormitory, taking notes on her clipboard as she went.

Finally, it was over. They each got a uniform violation and Marina got another check for an unmade bed and general messiness, but that was it. The dorm head shut the door behind her and Marina collapsed onto the couch with relief.

"Thank goodness. I thought she'd never leave. When did you get back? Did you sleep in Roxy's room?"

"Ugh."

Lulu flopped down on the couch next to Marina, throwing her hand over her eyes as she sprawled. "I just stayed there until she passed out and then left again. She's not going to get out of bed today. She kept me up until almost four, she was so hyper."

"I have a project to work on," remembered Marina. "I need to get that done today."

"Good luck with that, honey. I'm going to go get breakfast and then get back in bed. I'm exhausted."

"I think I'll just have some water and then go work out," said Marina, her stomach twisting as she remembered Rob's words from the night before. A part of her still thought it had just been an unpleasant dream.

"Were you okay last night?" Lulu asked as she stood up. "You seemed upset when we were leaving the party."

"Oh, yeah. Yeah I was totally fine. This guy just . . ."

Marina paused, wondering how much she should tell Lulu. Lulu was the one who'd told her she would stretch out her dresses in the first place, the one who had made her cry before this guy had upset her. Just because she was acting nice now didn't mean Marina could trust her.

"Yeah?" Lulu said, eyebrows raised.

"Nothing," Marina said, deciding on silence.

"Nothing. I felt a little sick from the daiquiris, all that sugar, you know, but I don't think I was upset about anything."

"I saw you dancing with that guy. He was pretty cute."

"Yeah, I guess. Not really my type, but he was a good dancer."

"I danced with a few boys, too," said Lulu. "One asked if he could give me a ride back here, but the rules are so strict I figured I wouldn't even be allowed to show up late at night in a boy's car. I might get expelled," said Lulu sarcastically, studying her nails.

"They're going to tell our parents we got strikes," said Marina.

"Yeah." Lulu didn't seem concerned.

Marina stood up, pulling her hair into a ponytail. Her mom wouldn't really care. She'd probably roll her brown eyes, laugh at Marina for being so messy, and leave it at that. Since Marina wasn't usually in trouble, she wouldn't mind this one transgression. Marina didn't think she would tell Marina's father, if he even asked about it. He was at the office so much that she didn't like to bother him when he came home.

"I've got to go on a run," said Marina. "I'm so bloated from all the drinks last night."

Just for a second, she saw Lulu's eyes narrow, as though she could see through Marina brushing off last night like nothing bad had really happened. Marina blinked, and the look was gone. Lulu shrugged, her pajama shirt sliding down one thin shoulder.

"You're crazy," she said. "I'm going to eat donuts."

With that, Lulu was gone, the front door slamming behind her. They didn't have to wear their uniforms on the weekend, just during inspections, so she wouldn't get in trouble at breakfast for being in pajamas. Marina sighed as she walked back into her bedroom, rubbing her temples. Her entire body felt like a balloon, completely bloated from the sugary drinks. She wanted to eat a huge plate of nachos, or spaghetti with meatballs, but Rob's words still rang in her head. Wavering, she considered her options.

Blowing off a run this once won't put me back that far,

thought Marina. *I drank a lot of those drinks but I didn't eat a lot. It was just fruit juice and stuff—there couldn't have been that many calories.*

Marina pulled out her laptop from its raspberry-printed case and opened Google to check how many calories were in fruity virgin daiquiris and energy drinks. Her heart sank as she read, and then it dropped into her stomach as she considered how many calories she'd actually had last night in liquid alone. She wasn't great at math, but she knew she was in trouble.

Marina closed her laptop, her heart pounding. She couldn't blow off this run now, no matter how much she felt like being lazy and lying in bed for the rest of the weekend with some snacks. Resolutely, she stood up and changed into yoga pants and a sports bra, quickly covering her stomach with an old, loose shirt. After grabbing headphones and choosing her favorite guilty pleasure station, Hannah Montana radio, she put her running shoes on and headed outside.

Just walking quickly down the hallway made her want to stop, as Marina's heart began to speed up and her breath came faster. Marina didn't look at any of the other residents, most of them talking as they headed to the dining hall for breakfast. Some of them glanced at her, and a couple that she recognized from her English class waved to her, but Marina didn't stop to chat. Instead, she weaved through the last part of the crowd and left out the side door of the dormitory into the sunshine. It wasn't quite spring yet, but the sky was blue and free of clouds, and the breeze was barely strong enough to be chilly. Marina breathed in the air and started to jog through the arboretum, winding along the trail that led all the way around campus. If she ran fast enough and far enough maybe she could just run away from this stupid body of hers that kept weighing her down. Her feet dragged in the dirt and she'd only been running for thirty seconds.

Come on. If you run for twenty minutes you can have pork chops tonight, Marina told herself. *It's not that much farther. Just a little bit farther.*

Chapter Eight

"Did you really sneak off to meet a guy in the bathroom at that party?" whispered Bridget to Marina on Monday as their professor droned on about Emily Dickinson.

"What?! No. Absolutely not."

"That's not what I heard," said Bridget. Marina tried to focus on the notes she was taking, but the teacher's voice was drowned out by what Bridget was saying.

"What did you hear?"

"That you danced with some guy all night, met him

in the bathroom, and then splashed a drink in his face. Is that part true?"

"Not really. I spilled some of my drink on him but I didn't, like, throw it in his face like in the movies."

"Girls?" Mrs. Riley paused her lecture to stare pointedly at Bridget and Marina. "Is there something going on back there that needs to be shared with the class?"

"No, Mrs. Riley," they chorused in unison.

Marina's cheeks flushed as everyone turned to look back at her, a few whispering behind their hands.

"I can't believe people are saying things like that about me," said Marina. "How did everyone hear about this?"

Bridget shot a glance at Marina.

"A bunch of girls saw Annabelle storm out of the dining hall. After that, everyone started talking about the whole thing."

"Great," muttered Marina. She didn't mind people knowing that she was out last weekend, not at all—but she didn't like the fact that they'd made

Annabelle mad. She wasn't nice even when she wasn't mad. Marina scribbled down a few more notes about symbolism in poetry, trying to keep up with what Mrs. Riley had on the board.

"You should all make sure to do the assigned reading before tomorrow's class," said Mrs. Riley. "Trust me on this one."

"Great, there's going to be another quiz," said Bridget. "We had one this morning in World History, too."

"Seriously?"

Marina hadn't looked over that reading material very carefully. On Sunday she'd exercised for a full two hours and then watched movies for the rest of the day before trying to look at some homework for the week. It was just hard to focus when all you could think about were stacks of brioche French toast.

"That's it for today, ladies. See you tomorrow, and don't forget about that reading."

Marina gathered her books and shoved them into her backpack a little more forcefully than was necessary. Monday was already proving more difficult than she'd anticipated.

Lunch was a little better than her morning had been. Marina allowed herself a bite of a glazed raspberry tart along with her cup of tuna salad, but that was it. As she ate though, she noticed Annabelle glaring at her from across the table. At least she thought she did. Every time she looked up from her tray Annabelle was chatting with the girls next to her, but every time Marina lowered her head, she could feel someone's gaze on her.

"Is Annabelle staring at me?" she whispered to Lulu next to her.

"I don't know," she answered, flipping her hair over her shoulder. "I don't think so. Why?"

"I don't know. I feel like she's mad at me."

"She's mad at Victoria, not you."

"She's never mad at Victoria for long, though."

They both watched as Annabelle leaned in next

to Victoria and laughed at something she said. It was true. She was never mad at her for very long; probably because Victoria just didn't really seem to care enough to actually get in a legitimate fight with her.

Lulu shrugged. "Whatever. Are you going to eat the rest of that?" She pointed to the remains of Marina's tart. Marina shook her head, and Lulu popped it into her mouth and smiled.

That night at dance practice, they began to learn the second half of the number that would be used in the auditions for the spring showcase. It was a contemporary piece, edgy and athletic, more likely to make Marina miss a step because of its difficulty level. She focused the entire practice, watching every move the girls in front of her made as well as Ms. Bennett, but she was always a beat behind. She leaned down onto her knees, sweating, as the instructor called for a break.

"Nice work, ladies," said Ms. Bennett. "Everyone take five and then we'll start again."

Marina's chest was heaving, and her legs were burning as she walked across the dance room to grab her inhaler. She took a deep breath and let her medication calm her inflamed lungs, her chest tight with worry. This piece was really advanced. The thought of doing it in front of all the seniors made her throat start to close.

"You're doing really well, Marina," said a sugary voice behind her, and Marina jumped as Annabelle appeared over her shoulder and smiled at her. Marina smoothed her hair back into her bun; Annabelle's was sleek and perfect, and Marina's was always threatening to spring from her bun into curls. Looking at Annabelle's made her feel like a frizzy mess.

"Um. Thanks?"

"Of course."

Annabelle smiled at her, another empty smile that looked brittle on her face, and then she walked away. Marina stood and took a swig from her water bottle, trying to act as though she weren't thrown by

Annabelle's words of encouragement. Why would Annabelle tell her she was doing well? First of all, Marina knew she was struggling with this dance, and second of all, Annabelle never complimented underclassmen. She never complimented, well, anybody, and meant it. Marina shrugged to herself. Maybe she was just jealous that Marina had gone to the party with her supposed best friend. It wasn't Marina's fault that Victoria hadn't wanted to wait until Annabelle could go. Surely she knew that.

"Alright, ladies. Let's run it again," called Ms. Bennett. Marina sighed, her stomach rumbling, and walked back onto the floor. She was going to be so sore after this practice.

By the time practice was over, Marina was too exhausted to care about showering in front of the rest of the girls. Her lungs ached, her stomach burned with hunger, and her legs were on fire. The sweat dripped down the muscles of her back and down her legs, and she couldn't bring herself to pull on clothes when she so badly needed a shower. Still, she waited in the locker room for a few extra minutes and pulled out her phone, pretending to check Twitter as girls showered and left so there would be less people around. Sweat dripped into her eyes and she irritably rubbed at the straps of her leotard where they were digging into her shoulders.

After a few minutes, she couldn't wait anymore to get out of her sweaty tights. Marina glanced around, then scurried into her corner and stripped before covering herself with a clean towel. No one seemed to notice. She walked into the shower area. There were ten marble stalls, separated by curtains, so at least they were individual—but she would still have to stand naked in front of everyone for at least a second before she got behind the curtain. Marina bit her lip, standing awkwardly in her towel, but the room was steamy and it didn't seem like anyone was watching. She walked in her flip-flops to an empty stall and double-checked; no one was inside, and there was soap, shampoo, and conditioner waiting on the shelves. In one swift motion, she hung her towel on the outside hook and stepped into the shower, drawing the curtain behind her.

Sighing with relief, Marina turned on the hot water and let it caress her tired muscles. There was definitely still extra weight around her middle, but her legs were slim and strong. It would be easier to appreciate them, though, if she had the same tight muscles in her tummy. Marina shampooed her thick hair and washed her body from head to toe until all traces of sweat were gone. As she washed, she worried. This dance was harder than she'd been prepared for. Contemporary was never her strong point; she was trained classically, in ballet, and the transition to the more modern movement of contemporary was something her body wasn't used to. She didn't have the muscle memory for the steps the way she did with ballet. In ballet, every dance was built on the same basic positions, whereas this style was completely new. She was still thinking about it when she turned the water off and squeezed her hair dry. Reaching around the curtain with one arm, Marina groped for her towel, but all she reached was empty air. Had it fallen down? Marina poked her head around the curtain, and her heart dropped into her stomach.

"Looking for this?" Annabelle stood in front of her, holding Marina's towel in her arms. On her face was a self-satisfied smirk, her bony hip was stuck out, and her nose was tilted in the air.

"What is wrong with you?" said Marina. "Give me my towel. It's cold."

"Why don't you come out and take it from me?"

"It's cold," Marina repeated, glancing around the shower room. There was no one else there that she could see, just Annabelle, but she didn't want Annabelle to see her naked. She didn't know what she was up to, but she knew it wasn't good.

"That's why you won't get out of the shower to get your towel? Because it's cold?"

"Lulu?" Marina called. "Ms. Bennett?"

"Stop yelling. Come and get your towel if you want it so badly."

"Why are you doing this?"

"I just think it's funny."

"What could be funny about this?" Marina was near tears and trying to hide it, still peeking around the curtain.

"I think it's funny that you're too embarrassed to come get this towel. We all see each other naked all the time. No one cares except you."

"So what? You're punishing me for being modest?"

"Oh, I don't think it's modesty. You always change in that stupid corner in the locker room, and I heard last weekend when you all went to that dumb party you threw a drink in some guy's face."

"That's not even true."

"But it's true you danced with him, isn't it? And it's true you got upset at something he said?"

Annabelle walked toward Marina, her lips twisting into a cruel sneer.

"It's none of your business what happened," said

Marina, trying to sound brave. "It's not my fault that Victoria wanted to go to the party without you."

Annabelle's pointed face turned red and blotchy with anger.

"I'm not stupid. I can put two and two together, here. Don't think I haven't been noticing your pathetic attempts to lose weight. You eat less at dinner and you're always working out, but it's not working, is it? Boys are still calling you fat, aren't they?"

Marina felt numb. She knew Annabelle was vindictive, but this was a level of cruelty she'd never expected. Knowing that Annabelle had been noticing her habits also made her skin crawl. She needed encouragement, not this. This made her feel even worse than Rob had made her feel at the party, and she hadn't thought that was even possible.

"I don't know what you're talking about," said Marina. "Look, just give me my towel back, please. I want to go back to my room."

"You're never going to be good enough at this dance to get a good slot in the showcase," said

Annabelle, and Marina felt another sickening bolt of shock shoot through her. Somewhere deep inside herself, she was terrified Annabelle was right.

"I never wanted you as an enemy," said Marina, her eyes filling with tears against her own will. "I just went because everyone else did. I didn't mean to hurt your feelings."

Annabelle scoffed. "Please. You didn't hurt my feelings. I just wanted to make sure you knew where your place really was in this school, and on this team."

"I never thought I was above anyone else."

Annabelle just rolled her eyes. Then she dropped Marina's towel on the floor and turned on her heels. "Nice talking to you. I hope you have a good rest of your night."

Then she was gone, the sound of her footsteps echoing as she left the locker room. Marina waited until she was sure she was gone, holding her breath to listen in case she was trying to trick her. Finally, there was no sound but the wheezing of her own breath. Marina stumbled from the shower on legs that had gone numb, groping for the towel Annabelle had dropped. She wrapped it around herself, sitting on the shower room floor, which she knew couldn't be sanitary. But she was past caring about that. Dropping her head onto her drawn-up knees, Marina began to cry—deep, heavy sobs that shook her chest and made her wish for her inhaler. All she could think was that she should be glad there was no one to witness what had just happened except for her and Annabelle. She could still see Annabelle's face twisted into a snarl, see her holding the white towel in her skinny arms. *Why would she be so mean?*

Marina's mind kept flashing back to the worst moments. Annabelle had noticed that Marina was struggling with tonight's number, and that definitely stung. Marina didn't always need to be the best, but she didn't want to be singled out as the worst. *How am I going to go back to dance practice again tomorrow?* Marina dabbed at her eyes with the towel, the water from her wet hair making a puddle around her. Annabelle was right. Boys would never look at her the way they looked at girls like Victoria, and even with the small amount of weight she'd already lost, she didn't feel like she looked any different. *It will take time,* Marina told herself. *You know it's going to take a while for the weight to come off, for the exercise to tone your muscles.*

But that didn't seem as comforting now. She wished there was some way to speed the process along, to show Annabelle that she was just as good as she was. Marina got up off the floor, her legs like jelly. She dried herself off with the towel, bundling her wet hair into a bun, and walked back to the locker room to put on her sweatpants and tank top. Marina walked out of the dance annex and into the night air, shivering a little as it chilled her wet hair and still-damp skin. Her eyes felt swollen and hot, and the cool air felt good as she walked to her dormitory. Marina checked in with the dorm head and then continued down the hallway to her room. Everything looked duller, less comforting than normal. Even her favorite paintings in the hallway, the one with the field of fuchsia tulips and the other of a red farmhouse against a backdrop of a mountain lake, didn't soothe her. The colors seemed jarring, off somehow—like Marina was stuck in a bad dream she couldn't wake herself up from.

Lulu was already in bed when she unlocked their door, and Marina went straight into her bedroom and shut herself in, turning the lock behind her. Then she switched off the light, crawled underneath her pink comforter and pulled it all the way up over her head. Closing her eyes, Marina tried to take slow and deep breaths. Her mom always said that she should let cruel words flow off her skin like water off a duck's back. It didn't need to affect her this much, or make her feel so helpless. More tears leaked out of the corners of Marina's eyes, and she ground her teeth in frustration. Easy advice for her mom to give, because she was perfect. Marina was tired, so tired, of trying so hard and getting nowhere.

You haven't been trying that hard, though, a voice in her head said. *You're still eating at least a few bites of dessert most nights. You could work out at least another*

98

hour a day, dance another hour, too, to get your weight down.

Marina considered that, lying alone in the dark. There was no way to control what Annabelle was going to say about her, or think about her. No matter what Marina did, she was the kind of girl who was going to spread rumors or be cruel for no reason, just to put her in her place. There wasn't anything she could do to stop her. But maybe she could prove her wrong. Maybe, if she doubled what she was doing now to lose weight, she could lose enough to really make Annabelle and everyone else realize she was serious. It was just so unfair that all the other girls at Beverly Hills Prep were all thin, or at least had cute little figures like Roxy, and Marina was stuck with this body that piled weight on her hips when she ate just a tiny bit more than everyone else. Why couldn't she be like Lulu, who could eat a thousand donuts and probably look exactly the same?

I guess I can't control that, either, thought Marina. *I can't help what kind of body everyone else has. I can't even control what kind I have.*

Rob's words at the party, Lulu's biting tone in the hallway about her hips, and Annabelle's venom from earlier all combined into a deafening chorus in Marina's head. She wanted it to end. This entire school was going to see what she was really capable of if she had to die trying.

Curling into a ball, Marina studied her ceiling in the dark. Enduring another episode like the one she'd gone through tonight was too much to bear. She'd rather never see another bowl of chocolate pudding in her life than have to go through that again.

Then do something about it, she told herself. *Something serious. Something that will make everyone look twice at you and reconsider everything they thought they knew about you. Don't just roll over and give up because Annabelle scares you.*

Marina lay in bed for half the night, letting Annabelle's words soak into her mind. She didn't try to forget about them, or deny them, or run from them. They reverberated in her head all night, and she let it happen. They wouldn't be her breaking point. They would be her motivation.

Chapter Nine

If Marina was watching her portions before, it was nothing compared to now. She began researching everything she put into her mouth before she chose it. She preferred arugula to spinach, but she forced herself to alternate between greens to keep her body from getting into a pattern. It was better to switch things up, keep her metabolism guessing—at least that was what she was reading.

"What book is that?" asked Bridget one evening as she slid into the seat in the library across from Marina.

"Is it something I'm supposed to be reading? Please say it's not. I'm already so behind."

"It's a book about health foods and which ones actually work," said Marina absently. "Did you know how much fat cashews have in them? It's enough to make me never want to eat another nut again."

"Okay," said Bridget uncertainly. "I'm going to study for our World History test."

"Oh, no," said Marina, setting the book down. "When is that again?"

"In like a week, I think."

"Okay. Then I have time."

Marina put her health book back up in front of her face, and Bridget shook her head. She couldn't understand why someone would care how much fat was in a cashew.

But Marina did. Mondays were designated as her meatless day, and she was allowed a serving of carbs on that day. Some of the articles she'd been reading swore that health drinks like smoothies or protein shakes were the way to go, but Marina couldn't bring herself to ingest liquid with such a high calorie count. Tuesdays she rewarded herself with meat as her protein, as long as the dining commons were serving something low in fat, or she just asked for sirloin steak strips on her salad. Wednesdays she ate an egg in the morning and then a lettuce wrap before dance practice. She ate whatever fish was on the menu for dinner on Thursday, and a few bites of green beans or some other green. Fridays she stuck to more greens and yogurt, and the weekends she sometimes ate nothing but eggs and dry toast.

The weekends were the hardest, when she had less going on to distract her from how hungry she was. Late at night, when Marina tossed in her bed and her stomach ached painfully, were her most vulnerable times. The nights had been the reason she started overeating in the first place; it was so much easier to sleep when you were stuffed with food and lulled into a comatose state. Now, she closed her eyes and tried not to think of turkey legs and gravy, of ice cream sundaes and milkshakes, and everything she craved but couldn't have. One night she dreamed she was eating a meatball sub and woke up with her sheets in her mouth.

Thursdays were her weigh-in days. Some people stepped on the scale every single day, her mom included, but Marina did it on Thursdays. It was a reward for her to step on the scale in the dance locker room and see a smaller number when she'd been dieting all week. Thursday was almost the weekend so it was an all-around positive time to do something as nerve-wracking as stepping on a scale.

At first, watching the number drop just gave her a glow of satisfaction. It was nice to see the rewards she was reaping from working so hard. But after the scene with Annabelle in the bathroom, Thursdays were different. She didn't look forward to them anymore so much as she just wished it was time to weigh in already, so she could start seeing results. The first week after Annabelle's torments, the scale had only dropped three pounds, and Marina had cried for two hours. After that, she strengthened her resolve even further, and the next week she more than doubled that number. It seemed a little crazy, even to her, but the weight couldn't come off fast enough. The more she lost the more she wanted to lose, like it was a contest she needed to win. After a couple weeks, it was like a game. The weight began to melt off, and she became so used to her diet that any time she ate more than three bites of anything she started to feel full.

And when she wasn't writing up a new day's diet plan, or measuring her waist with a measuring tape, Marina was in the studio practicing the audition piece for the showcase. Ms. Bennett, at her request, had given her a copy of the music, and agreed to unlock the dance room late so Marina could practice. Ms. Bennett came into the studio one Saturday afternoon to find Marina already there and sweating, working her way through the routine.

"Hi," said Marina, "I'm sorry. I didn't know you would need the studio today."

"It's fine, Marina. I just came in to catch up on choreography for some of the senior pieces. We can share the room."

Marina nodded, grabbing her inhaler and breathing in deeply. She'd already been here for two hours and she thought she could finally feel her body starting to get used to the dance. She took a swig of water and started at the beginning of the second eight count again, a section that had been giving her extra trouble. There was an aerial trick halfway through and she was slow on those; it took a lot of force to whip her legs over her head quickly enough to make the next beat. Marina took a deep breath and wiped the sweat from her brow absently, starting again, and she was unaware of the way Ms. Bennett's eyes followed her.

"Have you been losing weight, Marina?" she asked as Marina finished the eight count, landing the aerial cleanly.

"Um, yes," said Marina, taken aback at the direct question. "I mean, I've been focusing on eating a little healthier lately." She didn't know why she downplayed her efforts. It wasn't like she was doing anything wrong by being on a diet. God knows she could stand to lose the extra weight.

"You look good, don't get me wrong. Very good. You do seem a little thin, though, and so quickly."

"I seem thin?"

Marina looked down at herself. She was honestly surprised. Sure, the scale had been dipping steadily down in numbers for weeks now, but when she looked in the mirror she still saw a chubby girl who needed to slim her waist, with cheeks still plump with baby fat she was dying to lose. The pictures of models in the magazines she liked to read had prominent cheekbones and hollows in their face that Marina thought were so elegant. It was strange to hear that, to someone else, she looked thin.

"Yes, you do. You could stand to gain back a pound or two, even—again, in the best way."

"No offense taken at all," said Marina, her cheeks turning pink with excitement. Someone saying she needed to gain weight was the greatest compliment she could imagine at this point. "I didn't realize the weight loss was noticeable at this point."

"Well, it is. Very much so. I can see the straps of your leotard are just a bit loose."

Marina had noticed that. Her chest seemed to have shrunk lately, and where her straps normally dug in, now they were just as likely to slip from her shoulders.

"I'll have to order some in a smaller size," said Marina. "Ms. Bennett, since you're here, would you mind helping me with this eight count? I can't quite get the turn right after the pirouette. I'm always off balance."

She demonstrated, turning and then losing track of her spot during the second half of the motion. Ms. Bennett was struck again by how slim she was. Marina's legs, always rather slim, were genuinely tiny. Her fuller waist was trim and tucked. She didn't look so thin as to be alarming, but the change was certainly rapid and pronounced. Ms. Bennett chalked it up to her focus on the showcase. Marina wanted to look her best. That was something she couldn't fault. It would please her to see a few of the other girls show half as much dedication as Marina, in terms of the amount of time she spent practicing as well.

"You have your weight shifted too far backward," said Ms. Bennett, expertly judging Marina's form. "Have confidence in the motion. You're too worried about falling. Pick your spot and don't second guess it."

Marina tried again, finishing the move cleanly as she kept her spot and didn't shift her weight toward her heels. Ms. Bennett watched critically, nodding as Marina smiled.

"Again," Ms. Bennett said.

Ms. Bennett wasn't the only one who noticed Marina's new shape.

"You look really great, Marina," said Roxy as she sat down next to her in the dining commons. "Seriously. When did you get so skinny?"

"I'm not that skinny," said Marina, flipping

through one of her diet books. "I still have a lot of progress to make before I hit my goal weight."

"I can't even stop eating brownies long enough to think about a goal weight," sighed Roxy. Marina eyed her slim hips and rolled her eyes. Roxy was muscular from gymnastics and probably weighed one hundred pounds soaking wet.

"You don't need to lose any weight, Rox," said Lulu, echoing Marina's thoughts, as she sat down on the other side of Roxy. "You would disappear."

Roxy studied Marina critically, assessing the way her cheeks had lost some of their plumpness, and her hips were certainly less round than they had been. She sniffed, a little jealous, but she was still skinnier than Marina was. At least Marina had curves and didn't look like a walking praying mantis, all angles and harsh lines.

"Are you ready for the showcase auditions?" said Lulu, poking at her fried chicken. "I still mess up the last two eight counts every single time."

"I still mess up a lot, too," said Marina, but she

knew she was lying. The past few weeks she'd practiced that routine so often she could probably do it in her sleep. Ms. Bennett's advice had been the turning point; the help of her expert eyes did more than hours of practicing alone. Still, she occasionally did make a mistake. In front of the seniors, she wasn't sure how she'd perform. Pressure didn't do good things for her. It made her chest tighten, and made her asthma act up and her head spin. As much as she loved the spotlight, the minutes before she went on were agony.

"I'm sure you're both going to do great," said Roxy in her chipper voice, and Marina glanced up to see Annabelle looking their way from the head of the table. It seemed like her and Victoria had definitely made up, as usual, because she was sitting next to her. Her eyes narrowed in Marina's direction, and Marina quickly stared down at her carrot sticks. It still made her a little sick to look in Annabelle's direction, and even sicker to think Annabelle would be watching her audition in just a few days.

That night, Marina stayed in the dance studio until

past midnight, running through the routine over and over. She even allowed herself to forego her usual additional workout in favor of just dancing for an extra hour or so. This dance was athletic enough to count as cardio, anyway. Finally, the clock in the dance room passed midnight and Marina looked up in shock, dripping sweat onto the floor. Bending down, hands on her knees, she tried to catch her breath. Her legs were quivering, and her lungs were on fire. Marina walked off the floor to her bag, grabbing her inhaler. After practicing for so long, she felt as prepared as she could be for the audition. If nothing else, she was too tired now to keep worrying about it.

That's one thing about all this exercise, Marina thought, wiping sweat from her brow. *It really is a stress reliever.*

After this audition, she needed to pivot to worrying a little more about studying, though. Marina knew her schoolwork had taken a real hit with all the time she'd been spending rehearsing for the showcase audition and reading her dieting books and online articles.

There was a detox tea that looked promising that she'd already ordered, but she had no clue what reading she was supposed to have done tomorrow for English.

When this is over, I'll catch up, Marina told herself. *How hard can it be to do a little extra credit?*

She took the time to stretch out her muscles, making sure every bit of soreness was eased from her legs and back. Tomorrow was the audition. Tomorrow, she needed to be absolutely flawless. Turning off the lights as she left, Marina tugged up the strap of her favorite black leotard that had slipped down over her shoulder again. Her newer black one was tighter; she'd need to wear that one tomorrow, to make sure it didn't fall off. She'd weighed in tonight, and she was another five pounds down. It had been years since she weighed as little as she did now. It gave her a thrill to see the numbers go down lower and lower, but she wasn't satisfied. Not yet.

Chapter Ten

The morning of the audition, Marina woke too early. She couldn't sleep. Some of that was due to nerves, but more was due to her aching stomach. She pulled off her covers to look at her tummy, while still lying down on the bed. Her stomach looked almost perfectly flat; her hipbones poked out like points in a mountain range, sharper than she'd ever remembered seeing them. Poking at her tummy, though, Marina still imagined she felt the jiggle of nonexistent fat. All she could see were the pounds she had yet to lose. All she saw was more progress waiting to be made—not how far she'd already come.

Time to cut carbs entirely, thought Marina, tapping absently on one of her ribs. *Cut all carbs and stick to protein and veggies.* Launching herself from the edge of the bed, Marina dressed quickly into her uniform, noticing with some surprise how much the once-tight buttons on her chest had loosened. Using a safety pin to keep her plaid skirt from sliding down her hips, Marina grabbed her backpack and headed to breakfast. She could have a whole egg this morning—she would need the protein for later. The eight counts to the number repeated in her head over and over again as she walked, and Marina pictured every single move in her mind. Ms. Bennett sometimes said that picturing success was enough to make it happen. *I did more than picture it, though,* Marina thought to herself. *I worked for it.*

And I'll keep working for it, thought Marina. *I still have a long way to go.*

The locker room was almost completely silent that night as girls changed into black leotards and tights. There were some muted whispers, and competitive glances back and forth. Marina used hairspray in front of the mirror to make sure her bun was completely slicked back and that no hair fell free. The high bun pulled her cheeks taut, making her face nearly as slim as one of the models in her magazines. The realization filled Marina with pride, and also reinforced her decision to cut carbs from her diet. What she was doing was obviously working; the stricter she could be, the more calories she could cut, the better. It was like an addiction she couldn't get enough of now, watching the numbers fall off the scale.

Marina walked into the dance studio and began her warm-up stretches, spending extra time on her hamstrings and back, making sure she was limber. Annabelle already stood at the front of the room with her arms crossed, not even bothering to act like she cared about pretending to warm up with the rest of the seniors. Marina looked at her hands on her hips, her pinched face, and her mousy hair, and she remembered the night with the towel. She could still picture it if she let herself—the cruel way Annabelle's mouth had twisted, sneering at her, how completely humiliated Marina had been to be in such a vulnerable position. She never wanted something so much as she wanted to prove Annabelle wrong about the words she'd said to her that night. Marina slid into the splits, stretching her hip flexors. It was almost time.

"Alright, ladies. Let's run through the number a few times with everyone, including the seniors, and then we'll let the underclassmen have their turn."

Everyone hurried onto the floor. Marina found a spot near the center, a few lines behind the front.

"Remember, this is the night that underclassmen slots for the spring showcase are decided. The showcase itself is about five weeks away. So, nobody hold back. This is a time you want to be noticed, not blend into the crowd. Unless, of course, you're standing out due to mistakes."

Marina swallowed—around her she saw other underclassmen looking equally as panicked. Lulu was shaking like a leaf. Marina could see her a few spots down the line.

"Alright. I'll start the music. Everyone please get set."

Marina settled into the opening pose. This was just the practice round anyway, with all the seniors still on the floor. The music started suddenly, and Marina stumbled, nearly falling as everyone else began the first eight count. The music had started while she was distracted; she needed to catch up and focus. A rumbling sound came from her stomach, pulling her attention again, and Marina fought to get herself under control. The number ended and Marina walked in a tight circle, fanning her face and trying to act like she just needed air. Glancing around, she didn't think anyone had noticed her mistakes. The general atmosphere was so tight with tension that everyone seemed mostly concerned with their own performance, not hers. But when the seniors came to the front of the floor to watch, that would all change. The focus would turn to the underclassmen only, and Marina knew she'd been the subject of a lot of scrutiny lately. Was there anything more frightening than knowing everyone was going to be staring at her body, judging every move she made?

The music started again, and the second time around Marina's performance was much cleaner. She'd spent so much time training her body to anticipate the next step that even under pressure like this, her muscles seemed to know what to do as long as she relaxed enough to let her memory lead. Another round had her breathing harder, but she was warm now, limbered up and looser than she was in the beginning.

"Alright—seniors to the front," said Ms. Bennett, and Marina's heart skipped a beat. "Middle row, please come to the front."

Marina was in the middle row.

She stepped forward with her line to the very front

of the floor, just a few feet away from the seniors, who gathered into groups and folded their arms, giggling and whispering behind their hands. A drop of sweat trickled down Marina's back, and she took a deep breath. She was ready. This is what she'd been working for. Blocking out everything but the burning in her muscles, Marina waited for the music to turn on. When it did, she was ready—she leapt into the first eight count perfectly on time with the music, her muscle memory completely taking over. She didn't consider the move before she did it the way she usually did, which put her right on the beat instead of behind it. Her body knew what to do after the hours of rehearsal, and her mind was almost blank, her form effortless. She kept her weight forward on her turns and she marked her spot flawlessly. When the music ended Marina was almost surprised.

"Very nice," said Ms. Bennett, smiling pointedly at Marina. "Front row to the back, please, and back row come forward."

At least half of the seniors seemed to be staring at

Marina, especially Annabelle, who was glaring with a sort of furious scowl that made Marina swell with happiness. Annabelle would never look at her that way if she'd done poorly.

Marina practically skipped to the back of the dance floor, letting the former back row have their turn at the front. She danced better than she ever had in her life, the same eight counts over and over that were embedded deep in her body. Finally, Ms. Bennett had let every row have their turn in the front, and she called the practice. Marina immediately walked to the edge of the floor for water and her inhaler, dripping sweat. She was glad to see her hip bones poking against the fabric of her leotard. At least they were visible now, even if she had a long way to go before her tummy was as flat as she wanted it to be.

Marina walked in a circle to keep her muscles warm in case they needed to do the number again. Ms. Bennett was at the front of the room with the seniors, discussing who would be up for what part, and who would spend the most time onstage with the seniors.

Some underclassmen wouldn't be in the performance at all, Marina knew. There just wasn't enough space. And the spots that were available were precious. Most of them were just chorus positions in senior pieces, but you still got to be onstage. And there were a few lead roles for superior underclassmen—roles that actually gave a dancer solo time during the showcase even if she wasn't a senior. Marina had never considered that she might get a role like that, but when the seniors continued to look back and glance her way she felt hope swell in her chest like a balloon. A few seniors raised their hands as Ms. Bennett asked a question, and then Annabelle was the only one to raise her hand to another inquiry. Marina inched closer, trying to hear what they were talking about, but it was too late.

"Girls, gather around, please," called Ms. Bennett. "I'm ready to announce the parts for the showcase."

Marina took another quick puff of her inhaler before joining the group of girls milling to the middle of the dance floor.

"Everyone in this room impressed me tonight,"

Ms. Bennett began, glancing around the room. "I saw some truly remarkable performances. But, not every underclassman can have a part, and even fewer will have a solo part. Please keep in mind that the positions are limited, and know that if I had the room and time to give everyone a solo, I would."

She flipped a sheet back on her clipboard, and the entire room went still with anticipation. Marina jumped as her name was called, but it was for a standard position in the opening number; almost everyone got to be onstage for the opening act. The finale, though, was one of the most prestigious pieces to be in, even if you didn't dance a solo part. Marina closed her eyes and wished to hear her name, holding her breath with anticipation. *Please, please, let me get something. Anything.*

"Marina," she heard Ms. Bennett say, and Marina's eyes flew open. "I'm assigning you a brief solo part in the middle act, the Revival of the Swan Princess."

"Oh, my gosh," whispered Marina, as every face in the room turned toward her.

"Congratulations, Marina," whispered another second year, and a few others murmured the same. Annabelle, on the other hand, looked as though she'd just swallowed poison. That part alone was a huge honor, and a lot of pressure.

"I'm also assigning you a part in the final number, Marina," she said. "Not a solo—a chorus position."

Marina nodded, wordless with excitement. Her place in the final number would be longer than her solo, and in a smaller group she'd probably stand out just as much. In short, she'd been given another enormous role. She barely listened as the rest of the parts were given out. This was huge. This was everything she'd been working for.

That night, she left the studio feeling lighter than air. She went straight to her room and had two big glasses of water. As her stomach rumbled, she resisted the urge for even a snack. The pressure had only gone up from here. She still had a long way to go if she was going to be ready.

"Marina, baby, I'm so proud of you," gushed her mother over the phone when Marina told her the news about the showcase. "I haven't seen you in months, it feels like. I didn't even know you had the audition for the showcase already."

"I'm sorry, Mama," said Marina, sitting on a bench outside of the arboretum before her next class. She felt guilty; she usually told her mom every little thing, but she'd been so busy with her diet and practice that she hadn't spoken to her, except over text messages, in weeks. Marina checked her watch—she still had a few minutes to chat before she needed to get to class. A few freshmen on the dance team waved at her as they passed, then giggled and whispered when Marina smiled at them. She was something of a celebrity now with the younger girls. After all, she was only an under-classman herself, and she'd still snagged some huge roles for the biggest performance of the year.

"I saw a picture of you on Instagram that your roommate posted," her mom continued.

"You're friends with Lulu on Instagram? Jeez, Mom—that's so embarrassing."

"Why? She added me as her friend, or whatever you call it. I've seen more of you on there lately than I have in real life. You looked thin in the last picture, honey. You were all smiling in those cute little uniforms."

Marina knew the photo—Lulu had snapped it casually on the way to class. She had something like two thousand followers and thought that made her famous or something. No one had an Instagram like Victoria, though. Marina thought spending most of her summer abroad in Barcelona and on yachts had been cool, but Victoria's family spent time with actual celebrities and movie stars, and Victoria had her own boat that they took sailing off the coast of Greece. No one had more likes or more followers than Victoria did.

"I'm sorry I haven't called more," said Marina. "I was just so busy practicing for the audition and all that."

"I know, honey. It's okay. I did get some notice, though, about you being written up for a uniform violation? And something about messiness? I threw that one away. I know my own child is messy. Why that's something they need to write home about, I have no clue."

Marina laughed; she knew she could count on her mom to blow off that situation. A few checks for those kind of slight violations were no big deal.

"Anyway, Marina, please come home and visit this weekend. Your father should be here, and your brothers and sisters are dying to see you. I was thinking of having a little party, something to celebrate your big performance."

"The showcase isn't for a while, Mom."

"I know, I know, but the audition counts, too. Your aunts are already coming, and most of your cousins, plus a few of my girlfriends. And anyone you want to bring, of course."

Marina sighed. It was true, she hadn't been home in months, and it was just a party. She'd like to go home for a few hours at least and see everyone. As long as she stuck to her diet she'd be fine, and that wouldn't be too hard as long as she didn't stay long. Marina heard a bell ring from inside the school, and she jumped up from her bench, grabbing her backpack. As she started to walk to the door, though, she saw spots and heard a rushing in her ears. Her knees almost buckled, and then the feeling was gone. She straightened up again, reaching for the inhaler in the side pocket of her backpack. *That was weird. Maybe my blood sugar was low,* she thought. In that case, she'd just have to hang on a couple of hours, since she didn't have a snack scheduled until three this afternoon.

Marina put her inhaler back and continued into class, shivering a little even though the campus was bathed in sun. The other girls were starting to roll up the sleeves of their button-ups and Marina was still wearing the sweaters usually reserved for winter months. Maybe while she was home she could have her mom put in an order for uniforms for Marina in new sizes. The ones she was wearing were so loose that not even safety pins were enough to keep her skirt in place anymore.

Chapter Eleven

On Saturday morning, Marina woke up barely in time for room inspection, but luckily she'd cleaned her room the night before, so another check on her record wasn't necessary.

"You really have to go to this party?" said Lulu. She'd been extra nice to Marina ever since the showcase. All Lulu had gotten was a part in the opening, and almost everyone got to dance in the opening. At least Lulu didn't react the way Annabelle had when she'd gotten something Annabelle hadn't.

"Yeah. I haven't seen my family in forever. I'm

afraid my baby brother is going to forget who I am. And my little sister, too—I don't want her to forget who the boss really is."

"Are they the ones in the black and white photos on your Insta?"

"Yup," said Marina. She checked her watch; before she went home, a workout would be necessary. Afterward she was probably going to want to come home and pass out from the exhaustion of one of her mother's parties. It was strange not having to go to the dance room to practice the audition number, but she didn't need to do it over and over anymore. The audition was over; she'd done it.

Marina looked down at her tummy as she changed into workout clothes, and all she saw was progress waiting to be made. The audition might be over, but the work she'd need to do for the performance was just beginning. Marina pulled on a sports bra, almost loose on her frame now, and turned in her mirror. To her, she still had too full a chest, and a lot of fat to lose on her stomach. Even her legs weren't perfect, not yet. She didn't realize the mirror actually showed a girl with now-slender arms and a flattened chest, and a middle so thin that her hipbones gaped. Resolutely, she grabbed her headphones and set out for a run. An hour of cardio before the party would be a good start, then maybe another hour when she got back.

Marina's home was Mediterranean-style, white with blue edging, and everything inside was airy and open, perfect for warm California days. There was no carpet anywhere inside, only rich mosaic tile and hardwood, from the ten bedrooms to the outside infinity pool and zip line. Though the house wasn't especially close to the ocean, it wasn't a far drive—a few of her siblings surfed, so there were always boards stacked neatly at the house, next to the outdoor patio shower, but Marina had never liked it. She much preferred to enjoy the ocean when she was in it up to her knees, or lying on the sand and basking in the sun.

Her mom had sent a car, so Marina leaned back into the comfort of the front seat as one of their drivers took her down the highway toward home. Marina had chosen one of her favorite sundresses for the occasion, even though it bagged on her waist now and she had it safety pinned so it would stay on. It was light pink with gold edging on the bottom, tied at the back with a wide sash, which she'd double knotted so it wouldn't slip. The car pulled up to the wide double gates of her home, and the driver rolled down the window to speak into the intercom. With a loud clanging of metal, the gate swung to the inside to allow the car access to the long, looping driveway. Marina sat up now, leaning forward as her house came into view. A few of her siblings waited in the driveway already, running to the car even as the driver tried to shoo them away.

"Marina! Marina!"

As soon as she opened her door she was enveloped by a surge of bodies. Marina tried to see who was who, but then gave up and just opened her arms to everyone. Her youngest brother wasn't there, but he'd just learned to toddle so he wasn't exactly allowed in the driveway to greet her yet. It amazed Marina that her mother managed to keep track of them at all.

"Hi, everyone," she said. "Lupita, leave Amelia alone. No, don't pull her hair. Hi, Mark, I know—it's good to see you, too."

Then Marina's mother was at the front door, holding Marina's baby brother on her hip with one arm and wearing a Cartier diamond watch on the other wrist. Her hair was long and dark, curled like Marina's, and she had the same deep brown eyes and wide smile. Marina's heart swelled at the sight of her, her worries of the last few weeks falling away.

"Hi, honey! Welcome home! Okay, kids, everyone inside. I didn't raise you to scream in the driveway like savages."

She shooed everyone inside, handing off the baby to Marina's oldest brother George before enveloping Marina in a hug.

"So good to see you, Marina," she said, leaning back to look at her face. Her eyes widened, ever so slightly, as she held Marina away from her body and looked her over. "You've lost a lot of weight, baby."

"I've been dieting," said Marina. "And practicing a lot, you knew that. For the showcase audition."

"Of course," murmured her mother, spinning Marina in a circle, "but still. I didn't realize from that one photo all the weight you'd lost." A line of concern appeared between her eyebrows, one of the only signs of her age.

"It's not that big of a deal, Mama. I still have a ways to go, anyway."

"What? Marina, your dress is held on by a safety pin. You're thinner than I've ever seen you. There's no way you can get more weight off this tiny body," she said jokingly, but underneath ran a current of worry. Her baby loved to eat, always had, and had always been plump and happy. This slender girl standing in front of her, brown eyes huge in a face that was suddenly framed with narrow cheeks, was disconcerting, to say the least.

"I need to be ready to perform in the showcase," said Marina, and her mom nodded, letting the subject go, for now.

"Sure, honey. I don't want to make it seem like you don't look wonderful, because you do. We'll need to get you some new clothes, though, if you're going to keep this much weight off."

"I am going to," said Marina firmly. "I was going to ask you about that, though. I really need to go shopping."

"We'll plan a trip, and I'll go through the school to order you some new uniforms, too. Okay, enough chatter in the front yard. Everyone is waiting to see you."

She put her arm around Marina's shoulders, noticing the way she seemed to be grabbing mostly bone, and escorted Marina through the wide double front doors into the marble foyer. The house was already full of people, relatives and friends and business associates of her father's that Marina recognized from other gatherings. She leaned into her mom's embrace and let herself be taken around the enormous living area. Everything was open design, so the entire bottom half of the house flowed from one room into another, from the kitchen and cavernous dining room to the living room and the parlor, circling back to the breakfast nook and the outdoor patio. Marina greeted her father, who encircled her in his arms; her dad wasn't a man of many words, but he always had a smile for her, and she was so bombarded with questions from everyone else that she appreciated the moment of peace.

Aunts pinched her cheeks and commented on how thin she was. Cousins pulled on her dress and asked her if she was coming to play in the pool, and Marina grabbed her baby brother at some point from George and held him in her arms as he babbled happily, reaching up to pat her face with one sticky hand. The chaos was familiar and welcome, and so were the plates and platters of food on the long dining table. Marina had small plates of food offered to her a thousand times in ten minutes, and she could smell tamales all the way from the kitchen. On top of that, there were all of her favorites: spicy sausage and cheese, artichoke and jalapeño dip, rosemary bread with oil and vinegar, and all the makings imaginable for tacos and mini quesadillas on homemade tortillas.

Marina's mouth was watering when she got pinned into a conversation with one of her aunts close to the food table and she couldn't escape. The smell of the food wafted toward her, and it irritated Marina more than anything. Didn't they know how hard she'd been working to lose weight? Temptation like this was the last thing she needed.

"Marina," said her mom, appearing out of nowhere with a plate of food, "honey, I can take your brother. I made you a plate."

"No, thanks, Mama," said Marina, shifting her brother in her arms. "I'm fine holding the baby."

"Are you sure? I have all your favorites here. I even made my spicy bean dip for you. It's in the fridge."

"Mama, I said I'm fine."

"You can't hold the baby all day and not eat," her mother said, trying to joke with Marina, but Marina's eyes narrowed.

"Mama, come on. Leave me alone. I'm fine with the baby. I don't want anything right now."

Marina's mom stepped backward, taken aback at the sharpness of Marina's tone. This wasn't like her. Marina had the most mellow personality out of all her kids, always smiling and relaxed. This harshness wasn't like her, but now wasn't the time to get into it.

"Alright," her mom said, "whatever you want, honey."

She set Marina's plate on the granite counter in the kitchen and had it covered to save for later.

Two hours later, Marina felt like she'd explained the showcase and the audition a thousand times to twice that many people. She'd been congratulated and fawned over, patted on the back enough times to make her think she was going to topple over. Finally, the bulk of guests had filed out, leaving mostly close family behind. The house was still full, but at least it was people Marina was comfortable with.

"Come sit in the Jacuzzi for a while, honey," said her mom as the kids sprinted off in a swarm to put their bathing suits on for the pool. "Just for a little while, then you can go back to school. I know you have to get back to work on that project."

"What project?"

"Didn't you say in a text a while ago that you had a major project coming up? History, or something like that?"

"Oh, jeez."

Marina had blown off the research for that project for weeks. She'd been too busy reading her diet books or working out to bother with it. It was a partner project, and the girl she was paired with, Lori, had been messaging her for weeks asking her to meet. Marina pulled out her phone and sent her a quick message asking if she wanted to meet later today.

"Everything okay?" said her mom.

"Yeah, yeah it's fine. You're right, though, I do

have a lot of work to do for that project. It's due on Tuesday."

"Okay. Well, you can work on it this weekend. For now, put on your bikini and come and sit in the Jacuzzi with your mother."

She smiled at Marina, already in her swimsuit and wrap with a floppy hat to keep the sun off of her face. "Your old suits are in the drawer in your room. See you downstairs in a minute."

Marina climbed the tall, curving staircase, running her hand along the wide oak banister. A few of her siblings liked to slide down it, but the drop from the wide balcony on the second floor to the first was a long fall and their mother had forbid it a long time ago. Marina was content just to slide her hand on the smooth varnish and make her way up the steps. Her room was the third door on the right, the only one that was painted bubble gum pink. It made Marina smile to see it, and to see her mom had left everything else the way she liked it, from the rose-colored lampshade to the watermelon rug over the hardwood.

She pulled out one of her bikinis from the bottom drawer of her nightstand and locked the door while she changed; if she had a nickel for every time a sibling had barged in while she was half-naked, she'd be a millionaire. The first suit she tried slid right off her hips and onto the floor, so she switched to a string bikini that she could tie tight enough to stay on. Normally, she avoided wearing it because it showed so much skin and made her hips feel enormous, but today it looked almost modest. She tied the last tie around her ribs as tight as she could so it wouldn't go sliding anywhere, but she didn't have much chest to cover up at this point. Marina turned in front of the mirror, critically poking at her stomach, her thighs. Still so much weight to lose. Just because her clothes were finally beginning to fit differently didn't mean she was finished. She was still seeing pockets of fat that needed to be eradicated.

Marina pulled on a cover up and went back downstairs, letting herself out the double glass doors to the pool area.

"Want anything to drink, honey?" her mom asked,

143

grabbing a Diet Coke for herself from the outdoor fridge. "A soda?"

"A water would be great," said Marina, plopping down onto one of the lounge chairs next to her mother after she lay down her towel. Her siblings splashed and screamed in the deep end of the pool, and it made Marina smile to watch them. The nanny was bouncing her brother in the shallow end as he giggled. Marina's mother handed her the water bottle, leaning back into her own chair. Marina wiggled out of her cover up and dropped it next to her lounge chair; when her mother glanced at her, she had to stifle a gasp.

"Honey, I can count your ribs," she said to Marina, keeping her voice light. "I can see your hip bones."

"Not really," said Marina.

Marina's mother pulled her sunglasses down over her nose and studied her daughter. Marina was so thin she could almost see the bones in her sternum, like you might on a corpse. A sense of panic invaded her own chest, but she knew she needed to stay calm. Marina wasn't going to react to anger.

"I think your diet has gone on long enough, baby, don't you think? Don't you want to look your best for the showcase, and not be so bony?"

"I'm not bony, Mama. You're crazy. And yes, I do want to look good for the showcase, and that's why I need to make sure to keep watching what I eat."

"You haven't eaten all day. At least, nothing that I've seen."

"Please, Mama, just let it go. I'm fine. I know what I'm doing."

"Marina, I really think—"

"Mom, stop." Marina sat up on her elbows and glared at her mother. Why was she trying to sabotage everything Marina had been working for?

"I'm just saying, honey."

"Well, don't. It's my body, and like I said, I know what I'm doing."

Marina's mother bit back a response. Instead, she smiled, choosing to let it go.

"Okay. I'm sorry."

"It's okay," mumbled Marina, lying back on her

towel. She didn't know what her mom's problem was. Marina might be thinner than she ever had been, but that didn't mean she was going to stop dieting. That was her own business, and if Marina thought she had a ways to go, then that was her decision. Her mom was just being overprotective. Marina had everything under control.

As soon as Marina got back to school, after she'd begged off from one last attempt from her mom to take a plate of food with her back to Beverly Hills Prep, she went on another run. She needed to feel her legs burning and clear her mind before she got started on this stupid project. After showering off and changing into yoga pants and a sweatshirt, Marina texted her partner for the World History project, Lori, again and they agreed to meet in the library in a half hour, which was perfect timing for Marina to grab a snack and then head over there. The fact that she hadn't eaten all day didn't register; her stomach wasn't growling anymore, and she didn't even really feel like eating, but she knew she'd have to or she wouldn't be able to focus. All she wanted to do was sleep, actually, but she couldn't fail this project. It was worth forty percent of her final grade.

In the dining hall, Marina allowed herself one boiled egg and a single serving of spinach and cranberry salad, with no dressing. She ate slowly, but not to savor her food. Rather, each bite now felt like a betrayal to the goals she was working so hard to achieve. Food was the enemy. Food made you fat. It was a new challenge to see how little food she could eat to get through in a day. Every single day she was amazed at how little she actually needed. Marina set her tray on the counter when she was done and walked out, unaware that a group of resident freshmen started whispering as soon as she left.

"So she's down to three bites of salad a day?"

"That's insane."

Marina sat down in the library and pulled out her history book, sitting near a window where sunshine was pouring through. All the rooms were too air-conditioned, it seemed, because she shivered everywhere she went, even in her sweatshirts. Lori showed up, and thankfully she'd already done most of the presentation on her own laptop, so all Marina had to do was write down her own speaking parts and make sure she knew the facts on every slide about her topic. Nothing too difficult, but Marina was finding it harder than usual to concentrate. Even with the words on the screen in front of her, she lost her train of thought and stumbled over her phrasing. After a few hours, she rubbed her hands over her face and told Lori she had practice all day tomorrow. Maybe she was just tired. It had been a really long week, after all. It was just an hour or so into dinnertime, but Marina grabbed her backpack and went straight to her room. Exhaustion overtook her as she walked into her bedroom, and she lay face down on her bed and slept until the sun came up the next morning.

Chapter Twelve

By Tuesday morning, Marina thought she definitely had gotten a handle on her presentation. She'd practiced all day on Sunday, or at least she'd had the PowerPoint open on her computer while she read through a diet book explaining portion size compared to muscle mass and exercise level. Two workouts a day on Sunday and Monday, plus dance practice Monday night, quieted her mind and calmed her down; in the mirror on Sunday she was nearly convinced she had somehow gained back at least a pound. On the bright side, they'd begun learning the numbers for the showcase and Marina was thrilled.

Her costume for *The Swan Princess* piece was exquisite. She'd wear a snowy white leotard with a feathered tutu all edged in gold, and white feathered wings for her shoulders, topped off with dyed white dance shoes and a sparkling headpiece that partially covered her eyes and transformed her into the character. Marina couldn't wait for the first dress rehearsal when she could put it all on and not just wear it briefly for a fitting, as she had on Monday. Ms. Bennett's eyebrows had raised when she saw how much the costume would need to be taken in to fit Marina, but she'd remained silent. A few of the other girls, though, had started whispering; Marina had heard them in the background, Annabelle's voice especially. It didn't matter. They were just jealous she'd gotten the best part.

Marina walked into her World History class on Tuesday and sat down next to Lori, pulling her blazer tight around her.

"So, you're ready, right?" said Lori, leaning over to Marina. "You know your half of the presentation?"

"Yup," said Marina, opening her book on super

foods as she sipped her detox tea that had finally come in the mail. "I'm all set."

"Good, because I volunteered us to go today. I think we're last."

Marina felt a shudder of nerves, but it was fine. She was ready. Nodding at Lori, she continued reading and sipping her tea. Then, suddenly, it was their turn. Marina walked with Lori to the front of the classroom, standing as Lori got the presentation set up on the projector. Lori launched into the first part of the presentation, and Marina followed along well enough, but then the slide flipped. Lori glanced back at her as the whole room went quiet, and Marina knew it was her turn, but when she opened her mouth to speak, her mind went completely foggy.

"Um," said Marina, stalling for time, "um, so, to pick up where Lori left off . . ."

The words on the screen were really for note taking, but in a panic Marina read them off verbatim, trying to jog her memory. She knew what she was supposed to say—the words were there somewhere in her brain, but it was like there was a cloud over them and it was blocking her access. Marina read through the slide, then flipped to the next one, and remembered a few things she was supposed to say, but she knew she'd missed a huge portion of the presentation. She just couldn't seem to remember exactly what she was supposed to say. Hadn't she and Lori gone over this section?

Lori picked up again after Marina flipped to another slide, glaring at Marina over her shoulder. All Marina could do was stand there and pretend to be following along, but she felt completely lost. There were snickers and whispers from the room, and the teacher called for quiet before letting Lori continue. Then, out of the corner of her eye, Marina saw a girl pass something under her desk. There were more whispers, then a shocked gasp, and Marina turned to see another girl hand a phone to someone else. *What are they laughing at?*

"Hey, quiet down. What is that?"

The teacher, Mrs. Sampson, strode over to the desk

and held out her hand. Still giggling nervously, the girl handed over the cell phone. Mrs. Sampson took it, her brow furrowing as she studied the screen. The room went silent as she looked from the phone to Marina and back again. Marina's heart jumped and lodged right in the center of her throat. *What is on that phone?*

"Marina, can you come with me, please?" said the teacher, gesturing toward the door, and Marina stepped forward on legs that had gone numb. In the hallway she turned to Mrs. Sampson and was surprised to see concern in her gaze. She'd assumed she was in trouble for something.

"Look, I know I didn't do that well in the presentation—" Marina started, but Mrs. Sampson shook her head.

"It's, um, not about that, honey."

"Then what is it? What's on that phone?"

Marina didn't wait for her to answer; she took it from her grasp and looked for herself. Marina pressed a hand to her mouth. It was a photo of her from behind, changing in the locker room for dance practice. She was facing the wall, the way she always was, and leaning over to pull her leotard on. The photo wasn't explicit or inappropriate, at least not outwardly—it was blurry, and all that was really visible of Marina was her back. But she could count the knobs of her spine, and the bones of her pelvis were visible from the angle of the picture. She was leaning forward, probably pulling her tights on, so the boniness of her back was exaggerated to look almost grotesque. It looked like a Snapchat screenshot that was now being passed around to people.

"Oh, my gosh," said Marina quietly. "This is awful."

"I'm very sorry someone took this, Marina."

"It's not your fault. You can't even really tell it's me except for the hair, I guess."

"Do you have any idea who did this?"

Marina snorted; it wasn't like it was hard to guess.

"Annabelle Clemens," she said. "That's who it was."

"Are you sure?"

"Yeah, I'm completely sure. She's the only one who would do something like this."

"I'll let the headmistress know. She'll need to hear about this."

"Is that really necessary?"

"I'm afraid so. Come with me. We'll go there now. I'm sure she'll want to speak with you, too."

"Okay," sighed Marina, rubbing a hand over her face. This wasn't even her fault; it didn't seem fair that she had to go, too. But Mrs. Sampson told the class that she'd be right back, and then Marina followed her down the hallway and across campus to the administrative building that housed Headmistress Chambers's office. She'd been in here back when she was arguing to be taken off the waitlist, but since then she'd never been back. The double doors were still the same imposing wood, dark and somber. Mrs. Sampson knocked and a voice called out from within.

"You may enter."

Mrs. Sampson turned the double knobs and ushered Marina inside. Headmistress Chambers sat at her enormous desk, eyeglasses lowered onto her nose as she peered at them both regally.

"Mrs. Sampson? What seems to be the issue?"

Mrs. Sampson handed the phone to the Headmistress, explaining the events that had unfolded earlier that morning. Marina shuffled her feet, feeling awkward as the headmistress's gaze fell on her. *Those eyeglasses must have X-ray vision or something,* thought Marina, because it seemed as though the dignified woman could see right through her. Headmistress Chambers studied the phone, even using two fingers to zoom in on the screenshot, and then looked back up at Marina.

"You're certain this is you, dear?" she inquired. "The photo quality certainly isn't ideal for identity resolution."

"It's me," said Marina. "I always change in that corner of the locker room."

The headmistress nodded, setting the phone down on her desk.

"I'll call Ms. Clemens in here a little later and deal

with her separately," she said. "Thank you for bringing Marina in, Mrs. Sampson. If you'll excuse us now."

Mrs. Sampson glanced down at Marina and then left the room, shutting the door with a quiet click behind her. The headmistress studied Marina from her desk, leaning forward to gaze at her with her hands folded. She was wearing a brooch, Marina saw, that looked like it was studded with diamonds. She couldn't take her eyes off of it.

"If Ms. Clemens was the one who took that picture, she'll be dealt with," the headmistress began. "And I'm inclined to trust your judgment on that identity. Let's just say this won't be the first time Annabelle will have been brought in for this kind of . . . behavior."

"Thank you," said Marina. "I don't care that much, though, honestly. It's not like you can really see anything. Just my back."

"Yes, indeed. That brings me to the other half of my concern."

The headmistress leaned back slightly in her chair, still studying Marina with that penetrating gaze.

"What is it?" said Marina uncertainly. She felt like a bug under a microscope. "Am I in trouble?"

"No, you're not," said the headmistress. "But I'm going to have you speak with a counselor. I think you may be suffering from an eating disorder."

Marina laughed. "That's ridiculous."

"Is it? I have eyes, Marina. I've seen your weight plummet this year, and I've seen you engaging more with that group of girls that doesn't always lead to the most positive of behavior. This also isn't the first time this issue has been broached in my office."

"Someone else came to you saying that I might have an eating disorder?"

"Yes. A few of the staff exhibited concern. And it appears that concern may have been warranted, especially looking at this photo. This is disturbing, Marina. I think you might need help."

Marina shook her head, dumbstruck. "There's nothing wrong with me."

"Maybe. We'll let the psychologist decide that. You'll have a doctor's appointment scheduled as well, to make sure your physical state hasn't suffered harm. I'm having you meet with the counselor twice a week for the next several weeks, and I'll pay attention to what she recommends, Marina. The doctor will probably want to schedule follow-up visits as well. If either even so much as suggests hospitalization, or that you need to desist from physical activity, that will include dance as well."

"No," gasped Marina. "No, you can't. The showcase is coming up in just a few weeks. I have a solo, there's no way I'm going to miss it."

"Then don't miss any of these appointments."

The headmistress's austere demeanor softened, just briefly.

"I don't want to punish you, Marina. I certainly don't want to have to pull you from a school team that you clearly love. But I also can't allow you to pursue habits that might be unhealthy, even dangerous, while you're under the care of the school."

Marina sighed. She just wanted to go lie down. This morning had exhausted her, and these people were all crazy. She wasn't anorexic, she was just on a diet, for God's sake. She'd been fat before, so it wasn't like she'd gone from being thin to even thinner. But she was also scared that if she argued any more that the headmistress would make her stop dancing. If she missed dance, they'd give her parts to someone else. Marina forced a smile, making eye contact with the headmistress.

"I'll meet with the counselor," she said. "I promise. Just please don't make me stop dancing." *And don't try and make me start eating carbs*, she thought. They couldn't control what she ate, could they?

"I'll be keeping close tabs on that, and on you, Marina. And I'll have to call your parents and inform them of this meeting."

"Jeez," muttered Marina. After the way her mom had acted this weekend, she just knew she was going to totally freak out over this.

"You know the rules. They'll be made aware of the situation and of your appointments with the school psychologist, as well as the doctor."

Her mom was going to freak.

"Fine, fine," said Marina. "That's all fine."

"Alright, then. Your first appointment will be tomorrow at nine, so you'll have to miss class. It will be excused for medical reasons. Other than that, you can go, Marina. I'll be in touch."

"I can go to my next class?"

"Yes. Why?"

"I'm just worried about Annabelle," said Marina awkwardly. She usually passed her on the way to English Literature.

"Let me deal with Ms. Clemens," said the headmistress. "You'll be just fine. Let me know if you have any problems. And if you see this photo anywhere else, let me know as well. I'll have all the staff on high alert for cell phone violations."

"Yes, ma'am."

Marina gathered her backpack and left the office, shutting the door behind her. She could still see the picture in her head, count the knobs of her spine and visualize the sharp angle of her hips. To Marina, though, all she could focus on were the pockets of fat she still saw sitting just above her buttocks—*more weight just waiting to be carved off,* she thought, *like fat from a Thanksgiving turkey.*

Chapter Thirteen

The doctor came to the school infirmary to examine Marina that evening. Marina was surprised; she'd never had a doctor come to her before. The doctor weighed Marina and made notes on his clipboard. He listened to her heart, looked in her mouth, and probed her stomach. He also asked what seemed like a thousand questions.

"Have you ever suffered from an eating disorder?"

"When was your last period?"

"Do you feel fatigued, or very tired, most of the time?"

"Do you have trouble focusing?"

"Are you cold most of the time?"

"What was your last meal?"

Marina answered them as best she could, tapping her foot against her chair. She was anxious to leave and practice her solo number. Finally, the doctor sat down in the chair across from her, studying Marina carefully.

"Can I go yet?" asked Marina.

"No, you can't go yet. I'm sorry."

Marina sighed, checking her watch.

"Marina, I need you to look at me."

She raised her eyebrows, looking the doctor in the eyes. His gaze was disconcerted, but focused.

"I'm diagnosing you with anorexia."

"What?"

Marina tilted her head. That sounded serious. She certainly didn't feel like she had a disease or anything.

"It's an eating disorder characterized by extreme weight loss brought about by starvation methods, and also extensive calorie burning."

"I've been on a diet," said Marina. "That's all. And

I'm a dancer, so I can't really help the fact that I burn a lot of calories."

"Marina, if you don't bring your weight up, your heart could suffer permanent damage. Your brain, as well, actually, but your heart is what I'm most worried about right now."

"I don't have to stop dancing, do I?" said Marina anxiously.

The doctor hesitated.

"Not yet. But you're right on the edge, Marina. If your weight drops any lower I'm going to hospitalize you."

So she'd have to be careful about losing more weight. The thought made Marina feel sick. She still had so far to go, so much progress to make.

"I'm going to notify the headmistress of your diagnosis and present a treatment plan. You'll be weighing in with a counselor regularly, and if she at any time has concerns for your physical well-being, she'll call me. We expect you to follow the treatment plan, Marina."

Marina didn't know what to do. She didn't want

to agree, but what was she supposed to say? If she said no, they would make her stop dancing. That couldn't happen.

"Marina? Do you understand what I'm saying?"

"Yeah, I do."

"Do you have any questions?"

"Nope. Don't think so."

"Take my card." He leaned forward and held it out, and Marina grabbed it and stuffed it into the pocket of her sweater without looking at it.

"Your counselor will be in touch in the morning. She'll be sending me regular reports, and she'll go over my treatment plans with you. If all goes well, I'll examine you again in a few months, and not before then."

"Sounds good," said Marina brightly. "Can I go now?"

"Have you ever suffered from anorexia before?" the counselor asked, studying Marina over her clipboard.

She was supposedly a doctor, but to Marina she just seemed like an annoying woman who liked to ask a lot of unnecessary questions. She was also irritatingly plump, and it made Marina a little sick just to sit close to her.

"You've asked me that like a hundred times," Marina sighed, picking at her sweater. She'd been going to these appointments for three weeks now, and it just felt like the same thing over and over.

"I repeat certain questions to see if your answers ever change," said the counselor gently, "and sometimes they do change, if you recall."

"I guess."

"Have you gotten your period yet?"

Marina hesitated. "No, not yet."

The doctor had asked her that too, but she hadn't gotten it in months, as far as she could remember. They said it was a side effect of the fact that she was so thin, which sounded more dramatic than Marina thought was necessary. What girl missed having her period?

"I'm still worried about your grades."

"I'm working on that."

After the fiasco with her presentation in World History, Marina had been instructed that she needed to bring her grades up across the board—she was barely passing most of her classes. It was part of her "treatment plan." According to the counselor, one of the side effects of anorexia, *or just being thin*, Marina thought, was brain fog that made concentrating difficult.

"Has Annabelle been giving you any trouble?"

"Not really."

Since the ordeal with the Snapchat photo Annabelle had mostly ignored her, or she shot her scathing glares whenever she saw her, which was fine with Marina. Somehow, being friends with her and the rest of the girls had become less important as she continued to prepare for the showcase. Lulu still chatted with her occasionally when they were in their dormitory at the same time, but seeing as Marina was barely ever in the dining commons anymore she didn't see as much of the other girls.

Even at dance, Marina kept to herself and felt antsy whenever Ms. Bennett called for a break. She wanted to keep moving, keep practicing. It had become the most powerful addiction she'd ever known, next to her personal eating challenges. That was what Marina had begun to call them in her head. Her PEC's—how little food she could manage to eat in a day while maintaining her normal workouts and dance practices. It was completely exhilarating to push her body further than she ever would have thought possible. Once she didn't eat anything at all, just drank water, for nearly forty-eight hours straight before caving. She couldn't tell anyone, though—certainly not the counselor, or her mother, who had called Marina in a panic after the call from Headmistress Chambers. She wanted Marina to come home, take a leave from school, but Marina had fought her tooth and nail on that. If she was home, she wasn't dancing, and if she wasn't dancing, they'd give her solo away. Her mother had finally agreed to let her stay as long as she was seeing the counselor regularly.

"Please, Marina," she'd said. "Don't lose any more

weight. You're skin and bones, I saw you at home. At the very least just maintain the weight you're at, okay, baby? You're thin enough."

Marina didn't understand why no one saw her body the way she did. Every time she looked in the mirror she saw new places that needed to be toned, new areas to focus on cutting fat from. Her arms, her thighs, her stomach—always her stomach—all still needed work. For whatever reason, everyone else's view of her was skewed. That wasn't her problem, though. Her focus needed to be on the showcase, on practicing her solo and the finale, and on being as thin as possible before then. She just had to hide that from the counselor.

Marina did her required weigh-ins every week, and she kept a food diary that she falsified every single day. Her weigh-ins she worked around by sneaking into the office early and adding weight to the scale, just a pound or two, barely enough to keep from arousing suspicion. She always ate right before her meetings so she'd be as heavy as possible. The counselor knew her numbers hadn't gone up much, but she was convinced

Marina's weight loss was leveling out and would soon stabilize and then start to climb with continued treatment. Soon enough they'd realize she was still getting thinner, but by then it would be too late.

"Can I go yet?" Marina asked. "I'm going to be late for my third period class."

The counselor checked her watch, then nodded.

"Go ahead. And remember, we'll have a weigh-in next week."

Marina nodded and smiled, then rolled her eyes as she left the room. She shifted her backpack onto her other shoulder; lately she'd been getting bruises from the straps cutting into her arms. Ms. Bennett had blinked at them when Marina came into the room for practice last night, and they did look pretty bad.

"I'll make sure they're gone for the showcase," Marina assured her, and Ms. Bennett had looked for a moment like she was about to cry.

As Marina changed in the locker room for that night's practice, she kept earphones in even as she tugged on her tights and leotard. She faced the wall, same as she always did, or some nights she even went and changed in an individual bathroom stall since that photo had been taken. Everyone stared when she changed in her corner, now—she knew that pretty much everybody in this entire school had seen the picture Annabelle took. Annabelle hated her more than ever, now, since she'd gotten into trouble with Headmistress Chambers. Marina could tell by the way she always glared at her, like she had to bite her tongue to keep from tormenting her, but she'd been leaving Marina alone. *Headmistress Chambers would be intimidating even to someone like Annabelle,* Marina thought. *She probably threatened to kick her off the team if she kept picking on me.*

The dance practices were becoming more and more intense as the showcase drew nearer; it was less than a week away, and Marina was so nervous it was hard to eat even the little she did per day. She had her parts down perfectly, though. Instead of doing cardio, all she'd done for weeks was practice her solo number and her part in the finale. Her dreams were filled with white feathers and pirouettes, and even when she was forced to sit still in class she was running eight counts in her mind and tapping out rhythms with her fingers. There was nothing she thought of more than the showcase, and when the night came for final fittings she turned in the mirror in her white leotard and her feathered tutu and she watched her headdress sparkle in the lights, her eyes shining through the slits in the mask like black diamonds. The costume designer pulled the leotard tighter around her middle, shaking his head as he tugged at the material.

"I'm going to have to take it in again," he said. "It's already too loose. It'll fall off of her if I leave it."

"It's fine for you to take it in again, right?" said Marina. "It's not an issue?"

"No, it's not a problem. I can do it again. But you have to stay at a steady size until the showcase. I can't take it in when you're about to go onstage."

It was said with a smile, but Marina noticed Ms. Bennett listening to the conversation.

"Sorry about that," said Marina, smiling back, and

then she was cleared to change again. She left the dance floor quickly, afraid Ms. Bennett was going to ask about the costume. It was no secret that Marina was meeting with a counselor, and no secret she was thin. Marina was worried she was going to clue in on what was happening and do something silly. All Marina had to do was get away with her real diet plan until the showcase, and then maybe she could start playing along more convincingly with their own treatment plan. But definitely not now. Not yet.

When Marina showed up to her weigh-in the next week, the counselor was already there with her arms folded over her ample chest. Marina paused on her way in the door, taken aback at her presence. Checking her watch, she saw she was nearly twenty minutes early. She always came early, so she could make sure the scale was set heavier than it should be for her weigh ins.

"Hi," said Marina uncertainly. "Did we reschedule

our time or something?" Her voice was breathy. It made her tired just to walk down the hallway at this point. All of her energy was saved for dance; nothing else mattered.

"No. I came early."

"Oh," said Marina lightly, swinging her backpack onto a chair. "Okay, then."

"I know what you've been doing, Marina."

Marina looked over her shoulder with an innocent smile. "What are you talking about?"

"Get on the scale."

"Now? But we haven't even gone over all of our questions yet."

"Now, Marina."

Marina eyed the scale, and then eyed the counselor. It didn't look like she was going to have a choice. Marina shuffled over to the scale; her heart seemed to have trouble moving faster these days. In dance, even when she was exercising, it seemed slow, heavy as a boulder in her chest.

Marina stepped onto the scale—one foot, and then

the other. She heard the counselor's sharp intake of breath as she saw Marina's true weight, what she'd probably been suspecting but had thought she was wrong about.

"Marina," whispered the counselor, "you're done. You're off the dance team, and you certainly aren't participating in that showcase."

"Please," whispered Marina, looking at her feet. "You don't understand what you're doing."

"You are not at a healthy enough weight for physical activity. I'm amazed your heart hasn't given out yet as it is."

"I'm fine," insisted Marina. "I really am, I've just had a hard few days. I'm having a setback."

"When your dance instructor called me I knew I needed to double-check. What I was seeing and what the scale was reading wasn't adding up, and now I know why. You altered the scale's weight somehow."

"No," stuttered Marina, "no, it's just been a bad few days. I've been too nervous to eat much."

"Well, now you can focus on getting healthy.

You're off. I'm calling Ms. Bennett and letting her know, and you're meeting the doctor as soon as he's available for another evaluation."

The showcase was tomorrow night. Marina's family was coming. Her mom had front-row seats for all six of her brothers and sisters. She'd been working for this all year. This couldn't be happening. She wouldn't let this happen.

"Okay," said Marina. "Okay, I'm sorry, alright. I didn't mean to lie to you, or let this go so far."

The counselor softened.

"I know this has been a very difficult thing for you to accept," she said. "I know it's hard. But I'm just trying to do what's going to be best for you in the long-term here, Marina."

"I understand," said Marina sweetly. "Let me know when the doctor can meet, and I'll try to work on getting back on track."

"You need to do more than try. The doctor should be available to see you the day after tomorrow, and I want you meeting with me again tomorrow night."

That made things a little more difficult, but nothing Marina couldn't manage.

"Okay," she said. "I'll see you tomorrow, then."

"I don't want to have to hospitalize you, Marina, but if the doctor recommends it, I won't have a choice. At this pace, that's what his recommendation will be. If you want to avoid that happening, I suggest you start trying to change your attitude. I'll see you tomorrow, and I'll call Dr. Davity now and tell him we need him here as soon as possible."

"Thank you for all your help," said Marina, and then she grabbed her sweater and her backpack and she left, letting the door slam behind her. She had a lot to do in very little time.

Back in her room, Marina took out the doctor's note that he'd written to excuse her from class. Pressing that note to another piece of paper, Marina copied his signature in clear, bold strokes. The rest of the note she composed stated that she was healthy enough to perform in the showcase. Maybe Ms. Bennett was friendly with the counselor, but Marina was betting she wasn't as familiar with the good doctor. The rest of the dance team was meeting for an unofficial party to celebrate the showcase in a senior's room, but Marina didn't go. They would just stare at her, anyway. None of them really understood, and finally, she didn't care. When Marina finally went to sleep that night, she had a plagiarized signature and a note that, if it all worked out, would allow her to perform. She just had to cross her fingers that the doctor wouldn't be available to come in until the weekend. Marina slept with the note next to her pillow, and she dreamed of swan princesses and fairies lighter than air.

Chapter Fourteen

"Marina, why are you getting dressed?"

Marina, already dressed in her swan princess costume and settling the headdress onto her dark curls, turned to Ms. Bennett.

"Didn't you see the doctor's note?"

"No, I didn't see anything. The last I heard your counselor had pulled you from the show."

Ms. Bennett came forward, around the makeup artist and the costume designer, and took Marina's hands. Her eyes were warm and kind, and very concerned. Marina felt her breath catch in her throat, and she rubbed at her chest. Her heart had felt even more sluggish today, barely pounding at all, like she was just fading away into nothing.

"Marina, honey," said Ms. Bennett. "I know you're going through a hard time. I can see every bone in your body. It breaks my heart to watch you do this to yourself."

"Please don't," whispered Marina as other girls walked by, each of them glancing at her and trying to act as though they weren't staring. "I just want to dance. Okay? I just want to dance and then I can work on my problems. I have a doctor's note. He said just for tonight I'd be just fine."

Ms. Bennett took the note from Marina, sighing as she read through it.

"It's really this important to you?" she asked. "Are you sure you feel well enough? After this, Marina, no more. After this you need to rest."

"After this, I can," said Marina, her eyes filling for the first time. "I need to show everyone. I need to prove to everyone that I can do this."

Ms. Bennett studied Marina for another minute, concern etched onto her face, and she looked down at the note again while Marina's heart threatened to stop altogether.

"Alright," she said, and Marina smiled. "Alright, just tonight."

Her gaze fell onto Marina's bruised shoulders, her protruding hipbones, the angles in her face that had somehow gone from rounded to sharp as knives. Ms. Bennett smiled softly. "Break a leg."

"Thanks," said Marina, and when her instructor was gone she breathed a sigh of relief. The doctor couldn't see her until tomorrow. Her counselor thought her instructor knew she wasn't cleared to perform. But neither of them knew how far Marina would go for this night, how little she wouldn't do to make it onto this stage. At this point she didn't know what the limit was at all.

"Hey, Marina," said a voice, and Marina turned to see Lulu, dressed and ready for the opening number in her bluebird costume. "I just wanted to say good luck."

"Yeah, you too," said Marina smoothly. "You'll be great."

"I'm really nervous, but thanks. You, uh, you look beautiful." Lulu's gaze traveled over Marina, taking in her costume, her arms that looked more like spaghetti than muscle and bone.

"Thank you," said Marina, grinning, and Lulu smiled and then left, shaking her head. Everyone thought she was insane, and Lulu was beginning to think they were right. The girl was nothing but skin. Lulu shuddered; looking at her had been like looking at a talking skeleton. It was eerie.

Marina swiped blush on her cheeks and fluffed the feathers of her tutu. She turned in her habitual movement in the mirror, examining herself from every angle in the mirror. She would never go back to being the chubby girl, even though that was what they wanted. Marina heard the curtain call for the first number and she took a deep breath and headed for the wings to wait for her cue. Her muscles were stretched and warm, her tummy alive with nerves. Her hands and feet were almost numb, purple with cold as her body pulled blood and warmth inward to her internal organs. The ache in her chest intensified, her heartbeat slowing under her hands as Marina rubbed at the spot, trying to aid the place where it hurt.

Then the curtain went up, and the opening number was onstage. Marina could hardly breathe as she watched from her place offstage. It was almost time. It was almost her turn. Then the curtain dropped, the stage plunged into darkness, and Marina hurried out into her spot at point. There were a few seconds of quiet, where all she could hear was the thud of her heart in her ears. Other dancers got into place behind her, but all Marina watched was the curtain. It rose, and her melody began to play, the one she had memorized by heart these past weeks. Marina rose on her toes and began to dance, letting the rhythm flow through her body. The moves were perfect, effortless due to her countless hours of practice. The spotlight blinded her, but Marina didn't care. She moved to the next eight count, her heart thudding in her chest in slow, ominous beats. All she noticed was the thrill of the lights and the joy in her night's triumph. This was it. This was all she'd worked for.

Her heart stopped beating.

Marina stumbled, stepping accidentally onto another dancer. She faltered, missing a turn, and nearly fell again. Her heart seemed to be barely beating, as though it was fighting for leverage somewhere deep inside her. Breath escaped her lungs, but no more came in. No oxygen was coming into her body. Marina leapt into the final pose and held it by sheer force of will. The curtain dropped, and Marina dropped onto the stage in a dead faint, her headdress shattering on impact into a thousand pieces.

Chapter Fifteen

"Her blood pressure is much too low."

"Breathing seems stable."

"Someone get some oxygen over here, please!"

Marina was aware of the words, aware of hands all over her body. Frustrated, she swatted at them like flies. She bruised so easily now that she was going to be purple if they were so rough with her. Through blurred vision, she saw an IV needle in the crook of her elbow. Then there was darkness.

Marina opened her eyes slowly, painfully. This time there were white walls and white sheets covering her legs. She glanced down; the needle was still there, and a hospital gown. She was in the hospital. There was something over her nose; as she reached for it, her mother appeared, pushing her hand back to the bed.

"That's oxygen, honey. It's helping you breathe. Just stay calm. The IV is giving you fluids."

"How many calories are in an IV?" croaked Marina through her mask. Her mom's eyes filled with tears. She was wearing pink earrings, tiny diamonds.

"You're dehydrated. Your heart is in critical condition. You should be worried about being alive, not about an IV."

"I'm sorry, Mom," said Marina. "If it makes any difference at all, I'm sorry."

Her mom groped for her hand on the sheets, and squeezed.

"Why, Marina? Why would you do all this to yourself? For what? For a dance?"

Marina sighed, her eyes like lead. Part of her just

wanted to sleep, and sleep, and wake up and have all of this be a bad dream. Another part of her wanted to relive it over and over again.

"I'm sorry," she heard herself saying again, and then she slid back into nothing.

For a while, all Marina saw was darkness. Voices came in and out of her consciousness, and she felt herself stir a few times, but she always slid back into sleep. Her heart thumped slowly and heavily in her chest, like a gong that someone kept ringing. Finally, Marina heard her mom's voice, and her eyes fluttered open. Marina looked around the room, at the mint-colored walls and the strange machines she was hooked up to. Her mother was talking to a woman in a white coat in the doorway, and they both turned when they heard Marina shift on her starchy sheets.

"Marina, you're awake," murmured her mother. "This is Dr. Castellano. She's been taking care of you."

For a moment, Marina couldn't even recall why she was here. Then, it came flooding back to her: the performance, and how her heart felt as though it had stopped beating during her solo.

"What happened?" said Marina. She felt weak and tired, like an old woman.

"Your body was beginning to shut down," said Dr. Castellano. "That's why you collapsed at the showcase."

"How long have I been asleep?"

"The showcase was last night," said Marina's mother. "It's morning now."

Marina couldn't believe she'd been out so long.

"Your heart was literally starting to fail, its weakened state exacerbated by your physical activity. I'm amazed you were able to dance at all, honestly," said the doctor, concern in her eyes.

"I missed the finale," Marina realized. "I must have, if this happened during my solo."

"That doesn't matter, Marina," said her mother, but

Marina wanted to cry. All that work, wasted. Why had this happened?

"Marina," said the doctor, "we need to get you on a treatment plan for anorexia, today. Your body is sending a clear signal that it needs help, and I want to give you that help."

Marina wanted to keep denying everything, to keep pretending like she was okay, but she didn't have the energy. To her, her body still felt like it was too big and clumsy, but on a different level she knew this couldn't be normal. She should be able to dance and run and do all the things she wanted without passing out in the middle of a performance because her organs were shutting down. That wasn't normal, and what was funny was that normal was all she'd wanted to be in the first place. Everyone had seen what happened at the showcase. That was so embarrassing.

"I feel so ashamed," Marina whispered, and her mom reached out to hold her hand.

"You didn't do anything wrong," she said. "It's going to be okay, Marina, I promise you."

"I don't know how to start over," said Marina. "I mean, I don't know how to feel okay letting myself eat again, I guess. In a normal way."

"Let me help you with that process," said the doctor. "We'll take it a step at a time. The recovery program has a high success rate for anorexia remission."

Anorexia. It was so strange to hear the word said out loud, to even begin to admit it was something that may apply to her. Marina toyed with her sheets. It seemed like an impossible journey to begin, and she didn't even know that she was ready. Marina looked up into her mother's eyes, and she saw her mom's worry, and her fear, and she felt sick for causing it. But she also saw hope, and love. Maybe those were more important.

"A step at a time," said Marina. "I think I can do that."

THE END